"What's the Lion Game?"
asked Telzey of her captors.

"You're engaged in it now," was their answer. They hadn't told her the rul~~~ ~~~ ~~~ ~~~ at a psi should be able t~~~ ~~~

The game was p~~~ ~~~ ~~~nsit circuits of an entir~~~ ~~~ of giant mentalists wh~~~ ~~~ ~~~he civilized planets.

Telzey was a human and as such she was a test piece. She was either a pawn to be sacrificed or a wild queen who could make her own decisions. Either way, the loser would not be just one talented kidnapped Earthling . . . the loser would be a whole civilization and possibly a few peaceful planets as well.

Because the Lion Game was played for keeps by a race of high-power double-dealers.

THE LION GAME

THE
LION GAME

JAMES H. SCHMITZ

ACE SCIENCE FICTION BOOKS
NEW YORK

A serial version of THE LION GAME appeared in *Analog*,
copyright © 1971 by The Condé Nast Publications, Inc.

THE LION GAME

An Ace Science Fiction Book / published by arrangement with
the Estate of James H. Schmitz

PRINTING HISTORY
Ace edition / June 1982
Second printing / January 1985

ISBN: 0-441-48434-4

Ace Science Fiction Books are published by The Berkley Publishing Group,
200 Madison Avenue, New York, New York 10016.
PRINTED IN THE UNITED STATES OF AMERICA

1

There was a quivering of psi force. Then a sudden, vivid sense of running and hiding in horrible fear of a pursuer from whom there was no escape—

Telzey's breath caught in her throat. A psi shield had closed instantly about her mind, blocking out incoming impulses. The mental picture, the feeling of pursuit, already gone, had touched her only a moment; but she stayed motionless seconds longer. Eyes shut, pulses hammering out a roll of primitive alarms. She'd been dozing uneasily for the past hour, aware in a vague way of the mind traces of a multitude of wildlife activities in the miles of parkland around. And perhaps she'd simply fallen asleep, begun to dream.

Perhaps, she thought. It wasn't very likely. She hadn't been relaxed enough to be touching the fringes of sleep and dream-stuff. The probability was that, for an instant, she'd picked up the reflection of a real event, that somebody not very far from here had encountered death in some grisly form in that moment.

She hesitated, then relaxed the blocking shield to let her awareness spread again through the area, simultaneously extending a quick, probing thread of thought with a memory-replica of the pattern she'd crossed. If it touched the mind which had produced the pattern originally, it might bring a momentary flash of echoing details and further information—assuming the mind was still alive, still capable of responding.

She didn't really believe it would still be alive. The impression she'd had was that death was only seconds away.

The general murmur of mind noises began to grow up about her again, a varying pulse of life and psi energies, diminishing gradually with distance, arising from her companions, from animals on plain and mountains, with an undernote of the dimmer emanations of plants. But no suggestion came now of the disturbing sensations of a moment ago.

Telzey opened her eyes, glanced around at the others sitting about the camp fire in the mouth of Cil Canyon. There were eleven of them, a group of third and fourth year students of Pehanron College who'd decided to spend the holidays in Melna Park. The oldest was twenty-two, and she was the youngest—Telzey Amberdon, age fifteen. There was also a huge white dog named Chomir, not in view at present, the property of one of her friends who had preferred to go on a space cruise with a very special date over the holidays. Chomir would have been a little in the way in an IP cruiser, so Telzey had brought him along to the park instead.

In the early part of the evening, they had built their fire where the great Cil Canyon opened on the rolling plain below. The canyon walls rose to either side of the camp, smothered with evergreen growth; and the Cil River, a quick nervous stream, spilled over a series of rocky ledges a hundred feet away. The boys had set up a translucent green tent canopy, and sleeping bags were arranged beneath it. But Gikkes and two of the other girls already had announced that when they got ready to sleep, they were going to take up one of the aircars and settle down in it for the night, a good thirty feet above the ground.

The park rangers had assured them such measures weren't required. Melna Park was full of Orado's wildlife, but none of the animals were at all likely to become aggressive toward visitors. As for human marauders, the park was safer than the planet's cities. Overflights weren't permitted; visitors came in at ground level through one of the various entrance stations where their aircars were equipped with sealed engine locks, limiting them to contour altitudes of a hundred and fifty feet and to a speed of thirty miles an hour. Only the rangers' cars weren't restricted, and only the rangers carried weapons.

It all made Melna Park sound like an oasis of sylvan tranquility. But as it turned toward evening, the stars of the great cluster about Orado brightened to awesomely burning splendor in the sky. Some of them, like Gikkes, weren't used to the starblaze, had rarely spent a night outside the cities where nightscreens came on gradually at the end of the day to meet the old racial preference for a dark sleep period.

Here night remained at an uncertain twilight stage until a wind began moaning up in the canyon and black storm clouds started to drift over the mountains and out across the plain. Now there were quick shifts between twilight and darkness, and eyes began to wander uneasily. There was the restless chatter of the river nearby. The wind made odd sounds in the canyon; they could hear sudden cracklings in bushes and trees, occasional animal voices.

"You get the feeling," Gikkes remarked, twisting her neck around to stare up Cil Canyon, "that something

3

like a lullbear or spook might come trotting out of there any minute!"

Some of the others laughed uncertainly. Valia said, "Don't be silly! There haven't been animals like that in Melna Park for fifty years." She looked over at the group about Telzey. "Isn't that right, Pollard?"

Pollard was the oldest boy here. He was majoring in biology, which might make him Valia's authority on the subject of lullbears and spooks. He nodded, said, "You can find them in the bigger game preserves up north. But naturally they don't keep anything in public parks that makes a practice of chewing up the public! Anything you meet around here, Gikkes, will be as ready to run from you as you are from it."

"That's saying a lot!" Rish added cheerfully. The others laughed again, and Gikkes looked annoyed.

Telzey had been giving only part of her attention to the talk. She felt shut down, temporarily detached from her companions. It had taken all afternoon to come across the plains from the entrance station, winding slowly above the rolling ground in the three aircars which had brought them here. Then, after they reached Cil Canyon where they intended to stay, she and Rish and Dunker, two charter members of her personal fan club at Pehanron, had spent an hour fishing along the river, up into the canyon and back down again. They had a great deal of excitement and caught enough to provide supper for everyone; but it involved arduous scrambling over slippery rocks, wading in cold rushing water and occasional tumbles, in one of which Telzey knocked her wrist-talker out of commission.

Drowsiness wasn't surprising after all the exercise. The surprising part was that, in spite of it, she didn't seem able to relax completely. As a rule, she felt at home wherever she happened to be outdoors. But something

4

about this place was beginning to bother her. She hadn't noticed it at first; she'd laughed at Gikkes with the others when Gikkes began to express apprehensions. But when she settled down after supper, feeling a comfortable muscular fatigue begin to claim her, she grew aware of a vague disturbance. The atmosphere of Melna Park seemed to change slowly. Hints of cruelty and savagery crept into it, a suggestion of hidden terrors. Mentally, Telzey felt herself glancing over her shoulder toward dark places under the trees, as if something like a lullbear or spook actually might be lurking there.

And then, in that uneasy, half-awake condition, there suddenly had been this other thing, like a dream-flash in which somebody ran and hid from a dreadful pursuer. To the terrified human quarry, the pursuer appeared as a looming animal shape in the dimness, big, moving swiftly, but showing no details.

And there had been the flicker of psi energy about the brief scene. . . .

Telzey shifted uncomfortably, running her tongue over her lips. The subjective experience had been chillingly vivid; but if something of the sort really had occurred, the victim was now dead. In that respect, there was no reason to force herself to a quick decision . . . It might, after all, have been only a dream, drifting up in her mind, created by the mood of the place. She realized she would like to believe it was a dream.

In that case, what was creating the mood of the place?

Gikkes? It wasn't impossible. She'd decided some time ago that personal acquaintances should be off limits to casual telepathic prowling, but when someone was around at all frequently, scraps of information were bound to filter through. So she knew Gikkes had much more extensively developed telepathic awareness than the average person. Gikkes didn't know it, and couldn't have put it to use anyway. In her it was an erratic, unreliable quality which might have kept her in a badly confused state of mind if she'd been more conscious of its effects.

But the general uneasiness Telzey had sensed and that brief psi surge, fragmentary but carrying a complete horrid little story, could have come from Gikkes. Most people, even when they thought they were wide awake, appeared to be manufacturing dreams much of the time in an area of their minds they didn't know about; and Gikkes seemed nervous enough this evening to be manufacturing nightmares and broadcasting them.

But again—what made Gikkes so nervous here? The unfamiliar environment, the frozen beauty of the starblaze overhanging the sloping plain like a tent of living fire might account for it. But it didn't rule out a more specific source of disturbance.

She might be able to make sure by probing into Gikkes's mind and finding out what was going on in there. But she didn't want to do it. Gikkes simply wasn't very stable; and if she began prodding around in those delicately balanced complexities now, she could cause unforeseeable harm.

She glanced over at Gikkes. Gikkes met her eyes, inquired, "Shouldn't you start worrying about that dog of Gonwil's? He hasn't been in sight for the past half-hour."

"Chomir's all right," Telzey said. "He's still checking out the area."

Chomir was, in fact, only a few hundred yards away, moving along the Cil River up in the canyon. She'd been touching the big dog's mind lightly from time to time during the evening to see what he was doing. Gikkes couldn't know that, of course—nobody in this group suspected Telzey of telepathic talents. But she'd done a great deal of experimenting with Chomir, and nowadays she could, if she liked, almost see with his eyes, smell with his nose, listen with his ears. At this instant, he was watching half a dozen animals large enough to have alarmed Gikkes acutely. Chomir's interest in Melna Park's wildlife didn't go beyond casual curiosity. He was an Askanam white hound, a breed developed to fight man or beast to the death in pit and arena, too big and powerful to be apprehensive about other creatures and not inclined to chase strange animals about without purpose as a lesser dog might do.

"Well," Gikkes said, "if I were responsible for somebody else's dog, if I'd brought him here, I'd be making sure he didn't run off and get lost!"

Telzey didn't answer. It took no mind-reading to know that Gikkes was irritated because Pollard had attached himself to Telzey's fan club after supper and settled down beside her. Gikkes had invited Pollard to come along on the outing—he was president of various organizations and generally important at Pehanron College. Gikkes, the glamor girl, didn't like it at all that he'd drifted over to Telzey's group; and while Telzey had no designs on him, she couldn't very well inform Gikkes of that without ruffling her further.

"I," Gikkes concluded, "would go look for him."

Pollard stood up. "It would be too bad if he strayed off, wouldn't it?" he agreed. He gave Telzey a lazy smile. "Why don't you and I look around a little together?"

Well, that wasn't exactly what Gikkes had intended. Rish and Dunker didn't think much of it either. They were already climbing to their feet, gazing sternly at Pollard.

Telzey glanced at them, checked the watch Dunker had loaned her after she smashed the one in her wrist-

7

talker during the fishing excursion.

"Let's wait another five minutes," she suggested. "If he isn't back by then, we can all start looking."

As they settled down again, she sent a come-here thought to Chomir. She didn't yet know what steps she might have to take in the other matter, but she didn't want to be distracted by problems with Gikkes and the boys.

She felt Chomir's response. He turned, got his bearings instantly with nose, ears and—though he wasn't aware of that—by the direct touch of their minds, went bounding down into the river and splashed noisily through the shallow water. He was taking what seemed to him a short cut to the camp. But that route would lead him high up the opposite bank of the twisting Cil, to the far side of the canyon.

"Not that way, stupid!" Telzey thought, verbalizing it for emphasis. "Turn around—go back!"

And then, as she felt the dog pause comprehendingly, a voice, edged with the shock of surprise—perhaps of fear—exclaimed in her mind: *Who are you? Who said that?*

2

She'd had chance mental contacts with telepaths on other occasions. As a rule, she didn't try to develop them. Psi was a wide and varied subject; and she was rather new at it, and too busy at college at present to want to give much time to serious experimentation. Problems could arise easily enough without that. She might become aware of a situation of which others weren't aware; and then it wasn't always possible to ignore the situation, to act as if it didn't exist. But depending on circumstances, it could be extremely difficult to take effective measures, since she didn't intend to let it become generally known that she was a psi.

What appeared to have happened in Melna Park tonight had seemed likely to produce just such problems. Then this voice spoke to her suddenly, coming out of the night, out of nowhere. The encounter obviously had been as unexpected to the other telepath as to her. She didn't know whether it would lead to a further complication or the promise of support, but she wasn't inclined to reply at once. The fact that he—there'd been a distinct male tinge to the thoughts—was also a psi didn't necessarily make him a brother. She knew he was human; nonhuman minds had other flavors. His questions had come in the sharply defined forms of verbalization; he might have been speaking aloud in addressing her. There was something else she hadn't noticed in previous telepathic contacts—an odd filtered quality, as though his thoughts passed through a distorting medium before reaching her.

She waited, wondering about it. While she wasn't strongly drawn to this stranger, she felt no particular concern about him. He'd picked up her verbalized instructions to Chomir, had been startled by them, and therefore hadn't been aware of anything she was thinking previously. She'd now tightened the veiling screens of psi energy about her mind a little, enough to dampen out the drifting threads of subconscious thought by which an unguarded mind was most often discovered and approached. Tightened further, as it could be in an instant, it had stopped genuine experts in mind probing in their tracks. This psi was no expert; an expert wouldn't have flung surprised questions at her. She didn't verbalize her thinking as a rule, and wouldn't do it now until she felt like it . . . She decided the situation was sufficiently in hand.

The silence between them lengthened. He might be equally wary now, regretting his brief outburst.

Telzey relaxed her screens, flicked out a search thought to Chomir, felt him approaching the camp in his easy loping run, closed the screens again. She waited a few seconds. There was no indication of interest from the other psi; apparently, even when he had his attention on her, he was able to sense only verbalized thoughts. That simplified the matter.

She lightened the screens again. "Who are *you?*" she asked.

The reply came instantly. "So I wasn't dreaming! For a moment I thought . . . are there two of you?"

"No. I was speaking to my dog." There *was* something odd about the quality of his thoughts. He might be screening them in a manner she hadn't come across before.

"Your dog? I see . . . It's been over a year," the voice said, "since I've spoken to others like this." It paused. "You're a woman—young—a girl—"

There was no reason to tell him she was fifteen. What Telzey wanted to know just now was whether he also had been aware of a disturbance in Melna Park. She asked, "Where are you?"

"At my home. Twelve miles south of Cil Canyon across the plain, at the edge of the forest. The house is easy to see from the air."

He might be a park official. They'd noticed such a house on their way here this afternoon and speculated about who could be living there. Permission to make one's residence in a Federation Park was supposedly almost impossible to obtain.

"Does that tell you anything?" the voice went on.

"Yes," Telzey said. "I'm in the park with some friends. I think I've seen your house."

"My name," the disembodied voice went on, "is Robane. You're being careful. I don't blame you. There are certain risks connected with being a psi, as you seem to understand. If we were in a city, I'm not sure I would reveal myself. But out here . . . Somebody built a fire this evening where the Cil River leaves the canyon. I'm a cripple and spend much of my time studying the park with scanners. Is that your fire?"

Telzey hesitated a moment. "Yes."

"Your friends," Robane's voice went on. "They're aware you and I . . . they know you're a telepath?"

"No."

"Would you be able to come to see me for a while

11

without letting them know where you're going?"

"Why should I do that?" Telzey asked.

"Can't you imagine? I'd like to talk to a psi again."

"We *are* talking," she said.

Silence for a moment.

"Let me tell you a little about myself," Robane said then. "I'm approaching middle age—from your point of view I might even seem rather old. I live here alone except for a well-meaning but somewhat stupid housekeeper named Feddler. Feddler seems old from *my* point of view. Four years ago, I was employed in one of the Federation's science departments. I am—was—considered to be among the best in my line of work. It wasn't very dangerous work so long as certain precautions were observed. But one day a fool made a mistake. His mistake killed two of my colleagues. It didn't quite kill me, but since that day I've been intimately associated with a machine which has the responsibility of keeping me alive from minute to minute. I'd die almost immediately if I were removed from it.

"So my working days are over. And I no longer want to live in cities. There are too many foolish people there to remind me of one particular fool I'd prefer to forget. Because of the position I'd held and the work I'd done, the Federation permitted me to make my home in Melna Park where I could be by myself. . . ."

The voice stopped abruptly, but Telzey had the impression Robane was still talking, unaware that something had dimmed the thread of psi between them. His own screen perhaps? She waited, alert and quiet. It might be deliberate interference, the manifestation of another active psi field in the area—a disturbing and perhaps malicious one.

". . . on the whole, I like it here." Robane's voice suddenly was back; and it was evident he didn't realize there

12

had been an interruption. "A psi need never be really bored, and I've installed instruments to offset the disadvantages of being a cripple. I watch the park through scanners and study the minds of animals . . . Do you like animal minds?"

That, Telzey thought, hadn't been at all a casual question. "Sometimes," she told Robane carefully. "Some of them."

"Sometimes? Some of them? I wonder . . . Solitude on occasion appears to invite the uncanny. This evening —during the past hour perhaps—have you . . . were there suggestions of activities. . . ." He paused. "I find I don't quite know how to say this."

A shivering went over her skin. "There was something," she said. "For a moment. I wasn't sure I wasn't dreaming."

"Something very ugly—"

"Yes."

"Fear," Robane's voice said in her mind. "Fear, pain, death. Savage cruelty. So you caught it, too. Very strange! Perhaps an echo from the past touched our minds in that moment, from the time when creatures who hated man still haunted this country.

"But—well, this is one of the rare occasions when I feel lonely here. And then to hear another psi, you see . . . Perhaps I'm even a little afraid to be alone in the night just now. I'd like to speak to you, but not in this way—not in any great detail. One can never be sure who else is listening. . . . I think there are many things two psis might discuss to their advantage."

The voice ended on that. He'd expressed himself guardedly, and apparently he didn't expect an immediate reply to his invitation. Telzey bit her lip, reflecting. Chomir had come trotting up, had been welcomed by her and settled down. Gikkes was making cooing sounds

13

and snapping her fingers at him. Chomir ignored the overtures. Ordinarily, Gikkes claimed to find him alarming; but here in Melna Park at night, the idea of having an oversized dog near her evidently had acquired a sudden appeal. . . .

So Robane, too, had received the impression of unusual and unpleasant events this evening—events he didn't care to discuss openly. The suggestion that he felt frightened needn't be taken too seriously. He was in his house, after all; and so isolated a house must have guard-screens. The house of a wealthy crippled recluse, who was avoiding the ordinary run of humanity, would have very effective guard-screens. If something did try to get at Robane, he could put in a call to the nearest park station and have an armed ranger car hovering above his roof in minutes. That remark had been intended to arouse her sympathy for a shut-in fellow psi, help coax her over to his house.

But he had noticed something. Something, to judge from his cautious description, quite similar to what she had felt. Telzey looked at Chomir, stretched out on the sandy ground between her and the fire, at the big wolfish head, the wedge of powerful jaws. Chomir wasn't exactly an intellectual giant but he had the excellent sensory equipment and alertness of a breed of fighting animals. If there had been a disturbance of that nature anywhere in the vicinity, he would have known about it; and she would have known about it through him.

The disturbance, however, might very well have occurred somewhere along the twelve mile stretch between the point where Cil Canyon split the mountains and Robane's house across the plain. Her impression had been that it was uncomfortably close to her. Robane appeared to have sensed it as uncomfortably close to him. He'd showed no inclination to do anything about it; and there was, as a matter of fact, no easy way to handle the matter. Robane clearly was no more anxious than she was to reveal himself as a psi; and in any case, the park authorities would be understandably reluctant to launch a search for a vicious but not otherwise identified man-hunting beast on no better evidence than alleged tele-pathic impressions—at least, until somebody was re-ported missing. It didn't seem a good idea to wait for that. For one thing, Telzey thought, the killer might show up at their fire before morning.

She grimaced uneasily, sent a trouble glance around the group. She hadn't been willing to admit it, but she'd really known for minutes now that she was going to have to go look for the creature. In an aircar, even an aircar throttled down to thirty miles an hour and to a contour altitude of a hundred and fifty feet, she would be in no danger from an animal on the ground if she didn't take very stupid chances. The flavor of psi about the event she didn't like. That was still unexplained. But she was a psi herself, and she would have to be careful.

She ran over the possibilities in her mind. The best approach should be to start out toward Robane's house and scout the surrounding wildlands mentally along that route. If she picked up traces of the killer thing, she could pinpoint its position, call the park rangers from the car and give them a story that would get them there in a hurry. They could do the rest. If she found nothing, she could consult with Robane about the next move to make. Even if he didn't want to take a direct part in the search, he should be willing to help her with it.

Chomir would stay here as sentinel. She'd plant a trace of uneasiness in his mind, just enough to make sure he remained extremely vigilant while she was gone. At the first hint from him that anything dangerous was ap-proaching the area, she'd use the car's communicator to have everybody pile into the other two aircars and get off the ground. Gikkes was putting them in the right frame of mind to respond very promptly if they were given a real alarm.

Telzey hesitated a moment longer but there seemed nothing wrong with the plan. She told herself she'd better start at once. If she waited, the situation, whatever it was, conceivably could take an immediately dangerous turn. Besides, the longer she debated about it, the more unpleasant the prospect was going to look.

She glanced at Dunker's watch on her wrist.

"Robane?" she asked in her mind.

The response came quickly. "Yes?"

"I'll start over to your house now," Telzey said. "Will you watch for my car? If there's something around that doesn't like people, I'd sooner not be standing outside your door any longer than I have to."

"The door will open the instant you come down," Robane's voice assured her. "Until then, I'm keeping it locked. I've turned on the scanners and will be waiting." A moment's pause. "Do you have additional reason to believe—"

"Not so far," Telzey said. "But there are some things I'd like to talk about—after I get there." She didn't really intend to walk into Robane's house until she had more information about him. There were too many uncertainties floating around in the night to be making social calls. But he'd be alert now, waiting for her to arrive, and might notice things she didn't.

The aircar was her own, a fast little Cloudsplitter. No one objected when she announced she was setting off for an hour's roam in the starblaze by herself. The fan club looked wistful but was well trained, and Pollard had allowed himself to be reclaimed by Gikkes. Gikkes clearly regarded Telzey's solo excursion as a fine idea.

16

She lifted the Cloudsplitter out of the mouth of Cil Canyon. At a hundred and fifty feet, as the sealed engine lock clicked in, the little car automatically stopped its ascent. Telzey turned to the right, along the forested walls of the mountain, then swung out across the plain. She was now headed south, in the direction of Robane's house. What the park maps called a plain was a series of sloping plateaus, broken by low hills, descending gradually to the south. It was mainly brush country, dotted with small woods which blended here and there into dense forest patches. Scattered herds of native animals moved about in the open ground, showing no interest in the aircar passing through the cluster light overhead.

Everything looked peaceful enough. Robane had taken her hint and remained quiet. The intangible bubble of psi screens about Telzey's mind thinned, opened wide. Her awareness went searching ahead, to all sides. . . .

Man-killer, where are you?

3

Perhaps twenty minutes passed before she picked up the first trace. By then she could see a steady spark of orange light against a dark line of forest ahead. That would be Robane's house, still five or six miles away.

Robane hadn't spoken again. There'd been numerous fleeting contacts with animal minds savage enough in their own way, deadly to one another. But the thing which hunted man should have a special quality, one she would recognize when she touched it.

She touched it suddenly—a blur of alert malignance, gone almost at once. She was prepared for it, but it still sent a thrill of alarm through her. She moistened her lips, told herself again she was safe in the car. The creature definitely hadn't been far away. Telzey slipped over for a moment into Chomir's mind. The big dog stood a little beyond the circle of firelight, probing the land to the south. He was unquiet but no more than she had intended him to be. His senses had found nothing of unusual significance. The menace wasn't there.

It was around here, ahead, or to left or right. Telzey let the car move on slowly. After a while, she caught the blur for a moment again, lost it again. . . .

She approached Robane's house gradually. Presently

she could make it out well enough in the cluster light, a sizable structure set in a garden of its own which ended where the forest began. Part of the building was two-storied, with a balcony running around the upper story. The light came from there, orange light glowing through screened windows.

The second fleeting pulse of that aura of malevolence had come from this general direction; she was sure of it. If the creature was in the forest back of the house, perhaps watching the house, Robane's apprehensions might have some cause, after all. She'd brought the Cloudsplitter almost to a stop some five hundred yards north of the house; now she began moving to the left, then shifted in toward the forest, beginning to circle the house as she waited for another indication. Robane should be watching her through the scanners, and she was grateful that he hadn't broken the silence. Perhaps he realized what she was trying to do.

For long minutes now, she'd been intensely keyed up, sharply aware of the infinite mingling of life detail below. It was as if the plain had come alight in all directions about her, a shifting glimmer of sparks, glowing emanations of life-force, printed in constant change on her awareness. To distinguish among it all the specific pattern which she had touched briefly twice might not be an easy matter. But then, within seconds, she made two discoveries.

She'd brought the Cloudsplitter nearly to a stop again. She was now to the left of Robane's house, no more than two hundred yards from it, close enough to see a flock of small birdlike creatures flutter about indistinctly in the garden shrubbery. Physical vision seemed to overlap and blend with her inner awareness, and among the uncomplicated emanations of small animal life in the garden there was now a special center of mental emanation which was of more interest.

It was inside the house, and it was human. It seemed to Telzey it was Robane she was sensing. That was curious, because if his mind was screened as well as she'd believed, she shouldn't be able to sense him in this manner. But, of course, it mightn't be. She'd simply assumed he'd developed measures against being detected that were as adequate as her own.

Probably it was Robane. Then where, Telzey thought, was that elderly, rather stupid housekeeper named Feddler he'd told her about? Feddler's presence, her mind unscreened in any way, should be at least equally obvious by now.

With the thought, she caught a second strong glow. That was not the mind of some stupid old woman, or of anything human. It was still blurred, but it was the mind for which she had been searching. The mind of some baleful, intelligent tiger-thing. And it was very close.

She checked again, carefully. Then she knew. It was not back in the forest, and not hidden somewhere on the plain nearby.

It was inside Robane's house.

For a moment, shock held her motionless. Then she swung the Cloudsplitter smoothly to the left, started moving off along the edge of the forest.

"Where are you going?" Robane's voice asked in her mind.

Telzey didn't reply. The car already was gliding away at the thirty miles an hour its throttled-down engine allowed it to go. Her forefinger was flicking out the call number of Rish's aircar back at the camp on the Cloudsplitter's communicator.

There'd been a trap set here. She didn't yet know what kind of trap, or whether she could get out of it by herself. But the best thing she could do at the moment was to let other people know immediately where she was —

A dragging, leaden heaviness sank through her. She saw her hand drop from the communicator dial, felt herself slump to the left, head sagging down on the side rest, face turned half up. She felt the Cloudsplitter's engines go dead. The trap had closed on her.

The car was dropping, its forward momentum gone. Telzey made a straining effort to sit up, lift her hands to the controls. Nothing happened. She realized then that nothing could have happened if she had reached the controls. If it hadn't been for the countergravity materials worked into its structure, the Cloudsplitter would have plunged to the ground like a rock. As it was, it settled gradually through the air, swaying from side to side.

She watched the fiery night sky shift above with the swaying of the car, sickened by the conviction that she was dropping toward death, trying to keep the confusion of terror from exploding through her—

"I'm curious to know," Robane's voice said suddenly, "what made you decide at the last moment to decline my invitation and attempt to leave."

She wrenched her attention away from terror, reached for the voice and Robane.

There was the crackling of psi, open telepathic channels through which her awareness flowed in a flash. For an instant, she was completely inside his mind. Then psi static crashed, and she was jarred away from it again. Her awareness dimmed, momentarily blurred out. She'd absorbed almost too much. It was as if she'd made a photograph of Robane's mind—a pitiful and horrible mind.

She felt the car touch the ground, stop moving. The

slight jolt tilted her over farther, her head lolling on the side rest. She was breathing; her eyelids blinked. But conscious efforts weren't affecting a muscle of her body.

The dazed blurriness began to lift from her thoughts. She found herself still very much frightened but no longer accepting in the least that she would die here. She should have a chance against Robane. She discovered he was speaking again, utterly unaware of what had just occurred.

"I'm not a psi," his voice said. "But I am a gadgeteer —and, you see, I happen to be highly intelligent. I've used my intelligence to provide myself with instruments which guard me and serve my wishes here. Some give me abilities equivalent to those of a psi. Others, as you've just experienced, can be used to neutralize power devices or to paralyze the human voluntary muscular system within as much as half a mile of this room.

"I was amused by your cautious hesitation and attempted flight just now. I'd already caught you. If I'd let you use the communicator, you would have found it dead. I shut it off as soon as the car was in range—"

Robane not a psi? For an instant, there was a burbling of lunatic, silent laughter in Telzey's head. In that moment of full contact between them, she'd sensed a telepathic system functional in every respect—except that he wasn't aware of it. Psi energy flared about his words as he spoke. That came from one of the machines, but only a psi could have operated such a machine.

Robane never had considered that possibility. If the machine static hadn't caught her off guard, broken the contact before she could secure it, he would be much more vulnerable in his unawareness now than any ordinary nontelepathic human.

She'd reached for him again as he was speaking, along the verbalized thought forms directed at her. But the words were projected through a machine. Following them back, she wound up at the machine and another jarring blast of psi static. She would have to wait for a moment when she found an opening to his mind again, when the machines didn't happen to be covering him. He was silent now. He intended to kill her as he had others before her, and he might very well be able to do it before an opening appeared. But he would make no further moves until he felt certain she hadn't been able to summon help in a manner his machines hadn't detected. What he'd done so far he could explain—he'd forced an aircar prowling about his house to the ground without harming its occupant. There was no proof of anything else he'd done except the proof in Telzey's mind; and Robane didn't know about that.

It should give her a few minutes to act without interference from him.

"What's the matter with that dog?" Gikkes asked nervously. "He's behaving like . . . like he thinks there's something around!"

The talk stopped for a moment. Eyes shifted to Chomir. He stood looking out from the canyon ledge across the plain, making a rumbling noise in his throat.

"Don't be silly!" Valia said. "He's just wondering where Telzey's gone." She looked at Rish. "How long *has* she been gone, anyway?"

"Forty-two minutes," Rish said.

"Well, that's nothing to worry about, is it? She said she'd be gone about an hour." Valia checked a moment, added, "Now look at that, will you?" Chomir had swung around, padded over to Rish's aircar, stopped beside it, staring back at them with yellow eyes. He made the rumbling sound again.

Gikkes said, watching him fascinatedly, "Maybe

something's happened to Telzey?"

"Don't talk like that," Valia told her sharply. "What could happen to her?"

Rish got to his feet. "Well—it can't hurt to give her a call!" He grinned at Valia to show he wasn't really at all concerned, went to the aircar and opened the door.

Chomir moved silently past him into the car.

Rish frowned, glanced back at Valia and Dunker coming up behind him, started to say something, then shook his head, slid into the car and turned on the communicator.

Valia inquired, eyes uneasily on Chomir, "Know her number?"

"Uh-huh!" They watched as he flicked the number out on the dial, then stood waiting.

Presently Valia cleared her throat. "She's probably got out of the car and is walking around somewhere."

"Of course," Rish said shortly.

"Keep buzzing anyway!" Dunker said.

"I am." Rish glanced at Chomir again. "If she's anywhere near the car, she'll answer in a moment. . . ."

"Why don't you reply to me?" Robane's voice asked, sharp with impatience. "It would be very foolish of you to make me angry! Are you afraid to speak?"

Telzey made no response. Her eyes blinked slowly at the starblaze. Her awareness groped, prowled, patiently, like a hungry animal, for anything, the slightest wisp of escaping unconscious thought, emotion, that wasn't filtered through the blocking machines and could give her another opening to the telepathic levels of Robane's mind. In the minutes she'd been lying paralyzed across the seat of the aircar, she'd arranged and comprehended the multidetailed glimpse she'd had of it. She understood Robane very thoroughly now.

The instrument room of the house was his living area. A big room, centered about an island of immaculate precision machines. Robane had an aircar designed for his use but was rarely away from the house and the room. Telzey knew what he looked like, from mirror images, glimpses in shining machine surfaces, his thoughts about himself. A half-man, enclosed from the waist down in a floating mobile machine like a tiny aircar, which carried him and kept him alive. The little machine was efficient; the half-body protruding from it was vigorous and strong. Robane in his isolation gave fastidious attention to his appearance. The coat which covered him down to the machine was tailored to Orado City's latest fashion; the thick hair was carefully groomed.

He'd led a full life as scientist, sportsman, man of the world, before the disaster which left him bound to his machine. To make the man responsible for the disaster pay for his blunder in full became Robane's obsession, and he laid his plans with all the care of the trophy hunter he'd been. His work for the Federation had been connected with the further development of devices permitting the direct transmission of sensations from one living brain to another, and their adaptation to various new uses. In his retirement in Melna Park, Robane refined such devices for his purpose and succeeded beyond his hopes, never suspecting that the success was due in part to latent psi abilities stimulated by the experiments.

Meanwhile he prepared for the remaining moves in his plan, installed automatic machinery to take the place of his housekeeper and dismissed the woman from his service. A smuggling ring provided him with a specimen of a savage predator native to the continent, for which he'd set up quarters beneath the house. Robane trained the beast and himself, perfecting his skill in the use of the instruments, sent the conditioned animal out at night to hunt, brought it back after it made the kill in which he'd shared through its mind. There was sharper excitement in that alone than he'd found in any previous hunting experience. There was further excitement in treating trapped animals with the drug that exposed their sensations to his instruments when he released them and set the killer on their trail. He could be hunter or hunted, alternately and simultaneously, following each chase to the end, withdrawing from the downed quarry only when its numbing death impulses began to reach him.

When it seemed he had no more to learn, he had his underworld connections deliver his enemy to the house. That night he awakened the man from his stupor, told him what to expect and turned him out under the starblaze to run for his life. An hour later, Robane and his savage deputy made a human kill, the instruments fingering the victim's drug-drenched nervous system throughout and faithfully transmitting his terrors and final torment.

With that, Robane had accomplished his revenge. But he had no intention now of giving up the exquisitive excitement of the new sport he'd developed in the process. He become fully absorbed by it, as absorbed as the beast he had formed into an extension of himself. Every third or fourth night, they went out to stalk and harry, run down and kill. They grew alike in cunning, stealth and audacity, were skillful enough to create no unusual disturbance among the park animals with their hunt. By morning, they were back in Robane's house to spend most of the following day in sleep. Unsuspecting human visitors who came through the area saw no traces of their nocturnal activities.

During this period, Robane's scientific drive and skills had been concentrated on his goal. It seemed that presently then he began to expand his area of research again. Telzey could make out nothing clearly about that; a blurriness distorted what she had picked up. But Robane appeared to have become interested in psi machines in general as theoretical problems, and she had the impression he was working on a variety of projects at present, finding his only relaxation in the continuing frequent hunting interludes. Ordinarily, the killing of animals would satisfy him there. But he had almost no fear of detection now, and from time to time he remembered there'd been a special savor in driving a human being to his death. Then his contacts would bring another shipment of supplies to the house, and that night he hunted human game. Healthy young game which did its desperate best to escape, was run to the dropping point, and finally destroyed. Robane felt it was the least humanity owed him.

For a while, there'd been one lingering concern. During his work for the Overgovernment, he'd had contacts with a telepath brought in to assist in a number of experiments. Robane had found out what he could about such people and believed his instruments would shield him against being spied on by them. He wasn't entirely sure of it, but in the two years he'd been pursuing his pleasures and work undisturbed in Melna Park, his uneasiness on that point nearly had faded away.

Telzey's voice impression, following closely on his latest human kill, shocked him profoundly. But when he realized it was a chance contact, that she was here by accident, it occurred to him that this was an opportunity to find out whether a telepathic mind still could become dangerous to him. She seemed young and inexperienced —he could handle her through the instruments with the least risk to himself.

4

Rish and Dunker were in Rish's aircar with Chomir, Telzey thought, and a third person, who seemed to be Valia, was sitting behind them. The car was aloft and moving, so they'd started looking for her. It would be nice if they were feeling nervous enough to have the park rangers looking for her, too, but that was very unlikely. She had to handle Chomir with great caution. If he'd sensed fear in her, he would have leaped from the car and raced off in her general direction to protect her, which would be of no use at all. He was too far away at present.

Instead, he was following instructions he didn't know he was getting. He was aware of the route the car should take, and he would make that quite clear to Rish and the others if they turned off in any other direction. Since they had no idea where to look for her themselves, they'd probably decide to rely on Chomir's instincts.

That would bring them eventually to this area. If she was outside the half-mile range of Robane's energy shut-off device by then, they could pick her up safely. If she wasn't, she'd have to turn them away through Chomir again, or she'd simply be drawing them into danger with her. However, Robane wouldn't attempt to harm them

29

unless he was forced to it. Telzey's disappearance in the wildlands of the park could be put down as an unexplained accident; he wasn't risking too much there. But a very intensive investigation would get under way if three other students of Pehanron College vanished simultaneously, along with a large dog. Robane couldn't afford that.

"Why don't you answer?"

There was an edge of frustrated fury in Robane's projected voice. The paralysis field which immobilized her also made her unreachable to him. He was like an animal balked for the moment by a glass wall. He'd said he had a weapon trained on her which could kill her in an instant as she lay in the car; and Telzey knew it was true from what she'd seen in his mind. For that matter, he might only have to change the setting of the paralysis field to stop her heartbeat or breathing.

But such actions wouldn't answer the questions he had about telepaths. She'd frightened him tonight; and now he had to run her to her death, terrified and helpless as any other human quarry, before he could feel secure again.

"Do you think I'm afraid to kill you?" he asked, seeming almost plaintively puzzled. "Believe me, if I pull the trigger my finger is touching, I won't even be questioned about your disappearance. The park authorities have been instructed by our grateful government to show me every consideration, in view of my past invaluable contributions to humanity, and in view of my present disability. No one would think to disturb me here because some foolish girl is reported lost in Melna Park—"

The thought-voice went on, its rage and bafflement filtered through a machine, sometimes becoming oddly suggestive itself of a ranting, angry machine. Now and then it blurred out completely, like a bad connection, resumed seconds later. Telzey drew her attention away from it. It was a distraction in her wait for another open link to Robane's mind. Attempts to reach him more directly remained worse than useless. The mind stuff handled by the machines was mechanically channeled, focussed and projected; the result was a shifting, flickering, nightmarish distortion of emanations in which Robane and his instruments seemed to blend in constantly changing patterns. She'd tried to force through it, had drawn back quickly, dazed and jolted again.

Every minute she gained improved her chances of escape, but she thought she wouldn't be able to stall him much longer. The possibility that a ranger patrol or somebody else might happen by just now, see her Cloudsplitter parked near the house, and come over to investigate, was probably slight, but Robane wouldn't be happy about it. If she seemed to remain intractable, he'd decide at some point to dispose of her at once.

So she mustn't seem too intractable. Since she wasn't replying, he would try something else to find out if she could be controlled. When he did, she should act frightened half to death—which she was in a way, though it didn't seem to affect her ability to think now—and do whatever he said, except for one thing. After he turned off the paralysis field, he would order her to come to the house. She couldn't do that. Behind the entry door was a lock chamber. If she stepped inside, the door would close; and with the next breath she drew she would have absorbed a full dose of the drug that let Robane's mind instruments settle into contact with her. She didn't know what effect that would have. It might nullify her ability to maintain her psi screens and reveal her thoughts to Robane. If he knew what she had in mind, she would kill her on the spot. Or the drug might distort her on the telepathic level and end her chances of taking him under control.

"It's occurred to me," Robane's voice said, "that you may not be deliberately refusing to answer me. It's possible that you are unable to do it, either because of the effect of the paralysis field or simply because of fear."

Telzey had been wondering when it would occur to him. She waited, new tensions gathering in her.

"I'll release you from the field in a moment," the voice went on. "What happens then depends on how well you carry out the instructions given you. If you try any tricks, little psi, you'll be dead! I'm quite aware you'll be able to move normally again within seconds after the field is off. Make no move you aren't told to make. Do exactly what you are told to do, and do it without hesitation. Remember those two things. Your life depends on them."

He paused, added, "The field is now off."

Telzey felt a surge of strength and lightness all through her. Her heart began to race. She refrained carefully from stirring. After a moment, Robane's voice said, "Touch nothing in the car you don't need to touch. Keep your hands in sight. Get out of the car, walk twenty steps away from it and stop. Then face the house."

Telzey climbed out of the car. She was shaky throughout; but it wasn't as bad as she'd thought it would be when she first moved again. It wasn't bad at all. She walked on to the left, stopped and gazed up at the orange-lit screened windows in the upper part of the house.

"Look at your car!" Robane's voice told her.

She looked around at the Cloudsplitter. He'd turned off the power neutralizer and the car was already moving. It lifted vertically from the ground, began gliding forward headed in the direction of the forest beyond the house. It picked up speed, disappeared over the trees.

"It will begin to change course when it reaches the mountains," Robane's voice said. "It may start circling and still be within the park when it's found. More probably, it will be hundreds of miles away. Various explanations will be offered for your disappearance from it, apparently in midair, which needn't concern us now. . . . Raise your arms before you, little psi! Spread them farther apart. Stand still."

Telzey lifted her arms, stood waiting. After an instant, she gave a jerk of surprise. Her hands and arms, Dunker's watch on her wrist, the edges of the short sleeves of her shirt, suddenly glowed white.

"Don't move!" Robane's voice said sharply. "This is a search-beam. It won't hurt you."

She stood still again, shifted her gaze downwards. What she saw of herself and her clothes and of a small patch of ground about her feet all showed the same cold white glow, like fluorescing plastic. There was an eerie suggestion of translucence. She glanced back at her hands, saw the fine bones showing faintly as more definite lines of white in the glow. She felt nothing and the beam wasn't affecting her vision, but it was an efficient device. Sparks of heatless light began stabbing from her clothing here and there; and within moments Robane located half a dozen minor articles in her pockets and instructed her to throw them away one by one, along with the watch. He wasn't taking chances on fashionably camouflaged communicators, perhaps suspected even this or that might be a weapon. Then the beam went off, and he told her to lower her arms again.

"Now a reminder!" his voice went on. "Perhaps you're unable to speak to me. And perhaps you could speak but think it's clever to remain silent in this situation. That isn't too important. Let me show you something. It will help you keep in mind that it isn't all advisable to be too clever in dealing with me."

Something suddenly began taking shape twenty yards away, between Telzey and the house; and fright flickered through her like fire and ice in the instant it took her to realize it was a projection hovering a few inches above the ground. It was an image of Robane's killer, a big bulky creature which looked bulkier because of the coat of fluffy, almost feathery fur covering most of it like a cloak. It was half crouched, a pair of powerful forelimbs stretched out through the cloak of fur. Ears like upturned horns projected from the sides of the head, and big round dark eyes, the eyes of a star-night hunter, were set in front above the sharply curved serrated cutting beak.

The image faded within seconds. She knew what the creature was. The spooks had been at one time almost the dominant life form on this continent. The early human settlers hated and feared them for their unqualified liking for human flesh, made them a legend which haunted Orado's forests long after they had, in fact, been limited to the larger wildlife preserves. Even in captivity, from behind separating force fields, their flat dark stares, their size, goblin appearance and monkey quickness disturbed impressionable people.

"My hunting partner!" Robane's voice announced. "My other self! It is not pleasant, not at all pleasant, to know this is the shape that follows your trail at night in Melna Park. You had a suggestion of it this evening. Be careful not to make me angry again. Be quick to do what I tell you. Now come forward to the house!"

Telzey saw the entry door in the garden slide open. Her heart began to beat heavily. She didn't move.

"Come to the house!" Robane repeated.

Something accompanied the words, a gush of heavy subconscious excitement, somebody reaching for a craved drug . . . but Robane's drug was death. As she touched the excitement, it vanished. It was what she'd waited for, a line to the unguarded levels of his mind. If it came again and she could hold it even for seconds—

It didn't come again. There was a long pause before Robane spoke.

"This is curious," his voice said slowly. "You refuse. You know you are helpless. You know what I can do. Yet you refuse! I wonder . . ."

He went silent. He was suspicious now, very. For a moment she could almost feel him finger the trigger of his weapon. But the drug was there, in his reach. She was cheating him out of some of it. He wouldn't let her cheat him out of everything—

"Very well," the voice said. "I'm tired of you. I was interested in seeing how a psi would act in such a situation. I've seen. You're so frightened you can barely think. So run along. Run as fast as you can, little psi! Because I'll soon be following."

Telzey stared up at the windows. Let him believe she could barely think.

"Run!"

She whipped around, as if shocked into motion by the command, and ran, away from Robane's house, back in the direction of the plain to the north.

"I'll give you a warning," Robane's voice said, seeming to move along with her. "Don't try to climb a tree! We catch the ones who do that immediately. We can climb better than you can, and if the tree is big enough we'll come up after you. If the tree's too light to hold us, or if you go out where the branches are too thin, we'll simply shake you down. So keep running."

She glanced back as she came up to the first group of trees. The orange windows of the house seemed to be staring after her. She went in among the trees, out the other side, and now the house was no longer in sight.

"Be clever now," Robane's voice said. "We like the clever ones. You have a chance, you know! Perhaps you'll be the lucky one who gets away. We'll be very, very sorry then, won't we? So do your best, little psi. Do your best. Give us a good run!"

She flicked out a search thought, touched Chomir's mind briefly. The aircar was still coming, still on course —and much too far away still to do her any immediate good. . . .

She ran. She was in as good condition as a fifteen year old who liked a large variety of sports and played hard at them was likely to get. But she had to cover half a mile before she'd be beyond range of Robane's house weapons, and on this broken ground it began to seem a long, long stretch. How much time would he give her? Some of those he'd hunted had been allowed a start of thirty minutes or more. Half that might be enough.

She began to count her steps. Robane remained silent. When she thought she was beginning to near the end of half a mile, there were trees ahead again. She remembered crossing above a small stream flanked by straggling lines of trees as she came up to the house. That must be it. And in that case, she was beyond the half-mile boundary.

A hungry excitement swirled about her and was gone. She'd lashed quickly at the feeling, got nothing. Robane's voice was there an instant later.

"We're starting now."

So soon? She felt shocked. He wasn't giving her even the pretense of a chance to escape. Dismay sent a wave of weakness through her as she ran splashing down into the creek. Some large pale animals burst out of the water on the far side, crashed through the bushes along the bank and pounded away. Telzey hardly noticed them. Turn left, downstream, she thought. It was a fast little stream. The spook must be following by scent and the running water should wipe out her trail before it got here.

But others it had followed would have decided to turn downstream when they reached the creek. If it didn't pick up the trail on the far bank and found no human scent on the water coming down, it only had to go along the bank to the left until it either heard her in the water or reached the place where she'd climbed out.

They'd expect her, she told herself, to leave the water on the far side of the creek, not to angle back in the direction of Robane's house. Or would they? Angling back might be the best thing to try.

She went downstream as quickly as she could, splashing, stumbling on slippery rock, careless of noise for the moment. It would be a greater danger to lose time trying to be quiet. A hundred yards on, stout tree branches swayed low over the water. She could catch them, swing up, scramble on up into the trees.

Others would have tried that, too. Robane and his beast knew such spots, would check to make sure it wasn't what she'd done.

She ducked, gasping, under the low-hanging branches, hurried on. Against the starblaze a considerable distance ahead, a thicker cluster of trees loomed darkly. It looked like a sizable wood surrounding the watercourse. It might be a good place to hide.

Others, fighting for breath after the first hard run, legs beginning to falter, would have had that thought. . . .

Robane's voice said abruptly in her mind, "So you've

taken to the water. It was your best move."

The voice stopped. Telzey felt the first stab of panic. The creek curved sharply here. The bank on the left was steep, not the best place to get out. She followed it with her eyes. Roots sprouted out of the bare earth above her. She came up to them, jumped to catch them, pulled herself up and scrambled over the edge of the bank. She climbed to her feet, hurried back in the general direction of Robane's house, dropped into a cluster of tall grass. Turning, flattened out on her stomach, she raised her head to stare back in the direction of the creek. There was an opening in the bushes on the other bank, with the cluster light of the skyline showing through it. She watched that, breathing as softly as she could. It occurred to her that if a breeze was moving the wrong way, the spook might catch her scent on the air. But she didn't feel any breeze.

Perhaps a minute passed—certainly no more. Then a dark silhouette passed lightly and swiftly through the opening in the bushes she was watching, went on downstream. It was larger than she'd thought it would be when she saw its projected image; and that something so big should move in so effortless a manner, seeming to drift along the ground, somehow was jolting in itself. For a moment, Telzey had distinguished, or imagined she had distinguished the big round head held high, the pointed ears like horns. *Goblin*, her nerves screamed. A feeling of heavy dread flowed through her, seemed to drain away her strength. This was how the others had felt when they ran and crouched in hiding, knowing there was no escape from such a pursuer.

She made herself count off a hundred seconds, got to her feet and started back on a slant toward the creek, to a point a hundred yards above the one where she'd climbed from it. If the thing returned along this side of the watercourse and picked up her trail, it might decide she'd tried to escape upstream. She got down quietly into the creek, turned downstream again, presently saw in the distance the wood which had looked like a good place to hide. The spook should be prowling among the trees there now, searching for her. She passed the curve where she had pulled herself up on the bank, waded on another hundred steps, trying to make no noise at all, almost certain from moment to moment she could hear or glimpse the spook on its way back. Then she climbed the bank on the right, pushed carefully through the hedges of bushes that lined it, and ran off into the open plain sloping up to the north.

5

After a few hundred yards, her legs began to lose the rubbery weakness of held-in terror. She was breathing evenly. The aircar was closer again and in not too many more minutes she might find herself out of danger. She didn't look back. If the spook was coming up behind her, she couldn't outrun it; and it could do no good to feed her fears by watching for shadows on her trail.

She shifted her attention to signs from Robane. He might be growing concerned by now and resort to his scanners to find her and guide his creature to her. There was nothing she could do about that. Now and then she seemed to have a brief awareness of him, but there had been no definite contact since he'd last spoken.

She reached a rustling grove, walked and trotted through it. As she came òut the other side, a herd of graceful deerlike animals turned from her and sped with shadowy quickness across the plain and out of her range of vision. She remembered suddenly having heard that hunted game sometimes covered its trail by mingling with groups of other animals.

A few minutes later, she wasn't sure how well that was working. Grazing herds were around; sometimes she saw shadowy motion ahead or to right or left. Then there would be whistles of alarm, the stamp of hoofs, and they'd vanish like drifting smoke, leaving the section of plain about her empty. This was Robane's hunting ground; the animals here might be more alert and nervous than in other sections of the park. And perhaps, Telzey thought, they sensed she was the quarry tonight and was drawing danger toward them. Whatever the reason, they kept well out of her way. But she'd heard fleeing herds cross behind her a number of times, so they might in fact be breaking up her trail enough to make it more difficult to follow. She kept scanning the skyline above the slope ahead, looking for the intermittent green flash of a moving aircar or the sweep of its searchbeam along the ground. They couldn't be too far away.

She slowed to a walk again. Her legs and lungs hadn't given out, but she could tell she was tapping the final reserves of strength. She sent a thought to Chomir's mind, touched it instantly and, at the same moment, caught a glimpse of a pulsing green spark against the starblaze, crossing down through a dip in the slopes, disappearing beyond the wooded ground ahead of her. She went hot with hope, swung to the right, began running toward the point where the car should show again.

They'd arrived. Now to catch their attention—

"Here!" she said sharply in the dog's mind.

It meant: "Here I am! Look for me! Come to me!" No more than that. Chomir was keyed up enough without knowing why. Any direct suggestion that she was in trouble might throw him out of control.

She almost heard the deep, whining half-growl with which he responded. It should be enough. Chomir knew now she was somewhere nearby, and Rish and the others would see it immediately in his behavior. When the aircar reappeared, its searchbeam should be swinging about, fingering the ground to locate her.

Telzey jumped down into a little gully, felt, with a shock of surprise, her knees go soft with fatigue as she landed, and clambered shakily out the other side. She took a few running steps foward, came to a sudden complete stop.

Robane! She felt him about, a thick ugly excitement. It seemed the chance moment of contact for which she'd been waiting, his mind open, unguarded—

She looked carefully around. Something lay beside a cluster of bushes thirty feet ahead. It appeared to be a big pile of wind-blown dry leaves and grass, but its surface stirred with a curious softness in the breeze. A wisp of acrid animal odor touched Telzey's nostrils and she felt the hot-ice surge of deep fright.

The spook lifted its head slowly from the fluffed mottled mane and looked at her. Then it moved out of its crouched position—a soundless shift a good fifteen feet to the right, light as the tumbling of a big ball of moss. It rose on its hind legs, the long fur settling loosely about it, and made a chuckling sound of pleasure.

The plain seemed to explode about Telzey.

The explosion was in her mind. Tensions held too long, too hard, lashed back through her in seething confusion at a moment when too much needed to be done at once. Her physical vision went black; Robane's beast and the starlit slope vanished. She was sweeping through a topsy-turvy series of mental pictures and sensations. Rish's face appeared, wide-eyed, distorted with alarm, the aircar skimming almost at ground level along the top of a grassy rise, a wood suddenly ahead. *"Now!"* Telzey thought. Shouts, and the car swerved up again. Then a brief, thudding, jarring sensation underfoot—

She swung about to Robane's waiting excitement,

slipped through it into his mind. In an instant, her awareness poured through a net of subconscious psi channels that became half familiar as she touched them. Machine static clattered, too late to dislodge her. She was there. Robane, unsuspecting, looked out through his creature's eyes at her shape on the plain, hands locked hard on the instruments through which he lived, experienced, murdered.

In minutes, Telzey thought, in minutes, if she was alive minutes from now, she would have this mind—unaware, unresistant, wide open to her—under control. But she wasn't certain she could check the spook then through Robane. He'd never attempted to hold it back moments from the kill.

Vision cleared. She stood on the slope, tight tendrils of thought still linking her to every significant section of Robane's mind. The spook stared, hook-beak lifted above its gaping mouth, showing the thick twisting tongue inside. Still upright, it began to move, seemed to glide across the ground toward her. One of its forelimbs came through the cloak of fur, four-fingered paw raised, slashing retractile claws extended, reaching out almost playfully.

Telzey backed off slowly from the advancing goblin shape. For an instant, another picture slipped through her thoughts—a blur of purposeful motion. She gave it no attention. There was nothing she could do there now.

The goblin dropped lightly to a crouch. Telzey saw it begin its spring as she turned and ran.

She heard the gurgling chuckle a few feet behind her, but no other sound. She ran headlong up the slope with all the strength she had left. In another world, on another level of existence, she moved quickly through Robane's mind, tracing out the control lines, gathering them in. But her thoughts were beginning to blur with fatigue. Bushy shrubbery dotted the slope ahead. She could see nothing else.

The spook passed her like something blown by the wind through the grass. It swung around before her, twenty feet ahead; and as she turned to the right, it was suddenly behind her again, coming up quickly, went by. Something nicked the back of her calf as it passed—a scratch, not much deeper than a few dozen she'd picked up pushing through thorny growth tonight. But this hadn't been a thorn. She turned left, and it followed, herding her; dodged right, and it was there, going past. Its touch seemed the lightest flick again, but an instant later there was a hot wet line of pain down her arm. She felt panic gather in her throat as it came up behind her once more. She stopped suddenly, turning to face it.

It stopped in the same instant, fifteen feet away, rose slowly to its full height, dark eyes staring, hooked beak open as if in silent laughter. Telzey watched it, gasping for breath. Streaks of foggy darkness seemed to float between them. Robane felt far away, beginning to slip from her reach. If she took another step, she thought, she would stumble and fall; then the thing would be on her.

The spook's head swung about. Its beak closed with a clack. The horn-ears went erect.

The white shape racing silently down the slope seemed unreal for a moment, something she imagined. She knew Chomir was approaching; she hadn't realized he was so near. She couldn't see the aircar's lights in the starblaze above, but it might be there. If they had followed the dog after he leaped out of the car, if they hadn't lost him—

Chomir could threaten and circle Robane's beast, perhaps draw it away from her, keep it occupied for minutes. She drove a command at him—another, quickly and anxiously, because he hadn't checked in the least; tried to slip into his mind and knew suddenly that Chomir, coming in silent fury, wasn't going to be checked or slowed or controlled by anything she did. The goblin uttered a monstrous squalling scream of astounded rage as the strange white animal closed the last twenty yards between them; then it leaped aside with its horrid ease. Sick with dismay, Telzey saw the great forelimb flash from the cloak, strike with spread talons. The thudding blow caught Chomir, spun him around, sent him rolling over the ground. The spook sprang again to come down on its reckless assailant. But the dog was on his feet and away before it reached him.

It was Chomir's first serious fight. But he came of generations of ancestors who had fought one another and other animals and armed men in the arenas of Askanam. Their battle cunning was stamped into his genes. He had made one mistake, a very nearly fatal one, in hurtling in at a dead run on an unknown opponent. Almost within seconds, it became apparent that he was making no more mistakes.

Telzey saw it through a shifting blur of exhaustion. As big a dog as Chomir was, the squalling goblin must weight nearly five times as much, looked ten times bigger with its fur mane bristling about it. Its kind had been forest horrors to the early settlers. Its forefeet were tipped with claws longer than her hands and the curved beak could shear through muscle and bone like a sword. She'd seen its uncanny speed.

Now somehow it seemed slow. As it sprang, slashing down, something low and white flowed around and about it with silent purpose. Telzey understood it then. The spook as a natural killer, designed by nature to deal efficiently with its prey. Chomir's breed were killers developed by man to deal efficiently with other killers.

He seemed locked to the beast for an instant, high on its shoulder, and she saw the wide dark stain on his flank where the spook's talons had struck. He shook himself savagely. There was an ugly snapping sound. The spook shrieked like a huge bird. She saw the two animals locked together again, then the spook rolling over the ground, the white shape rolling with it, slipping away, slipping back. There was another shriek. The spook rolled into a cluster of bushes. Chomir followed it in.

A white circle of light settled on the thrashing vegetation, shifted over to her. She looked up, saw Rish's car gliding down through the air, heard voices calling her name—

And now, suddenly, there was all the time in the world.

She followed her contact thoughts back to Robane's mind, spreading out through it, sensing at once the frantic grip of his hands on the instrument controls. For Robane, time was running out quickly. He'd been trying to turn his beast away from the dog, force it to destroy the human being who could expose him. He'd been unable to do it. He was in terrible fear. But he could accomplish no more through the spook. She felt his sudden decision to break contact with the animal to avoid the one experience he'd always shunned—going down with another mind into the shuddering agony of death.

His right hand released the control it was clutching, reached toward a switch.

"No," Telzey said softly to the reaching hand.

It dropped to the instrument board. After a moment, it knotted, twisted about, began to lift again.

"No."

Now it lay still. She considered. There was time enough. Robane believed he would die with the spook if he couldn't get away from it in time. And because he believed it, he might—if it came to that.

But it wouldn't come to that.

There were things she still had to find out from Robane. The identity of the gang which had supplied him with human game was one; somebody should be doing something about those people presently. Then there were obscure aspects to his recent work with psi machines, suggesting he'd had associates in that, that there might even be a sizable secret project involved. It could be of significance. She had to study Robane further, another time.

She released his hand. It leaped to the switch, pulled it back. He gave a great gasp of relief.

For a moment, Telzey was busy. A needle of psi energy flicked knowingly up and down channels, touching here, there, shriveling, cutting, blocking. . . Then it was done, Robane, half his mind gone in an instant, unaware of it, smiled blankly at the instrument panel in front of him. He'd live on here, dimmed and harmless, cared for by a machine, unwitting custodian of memories that needed investigating.

"I'll be back," Telzey told the smiling, dull thing, and left it.

She found herself standing on the slope. It had taken only a moment after all. Dunker and Valia were running toward her. Rish had just climbed out of the aircar settled forty feet away, its searchbeam fixed on the thicket where the spook's body jerked back and forth as Chomir, jaws locked on its crushed neck, shook the last vestiges of life from it with methodical fury.

6

Three weeks passed before Telzey returned to Robane's house.

Her encounter with the spook created very little stir. She'd asked her companions not to talk about it, on the ground that it would upset her family if they learned she'd been in danger. Some of the group felt it was a shame to keep so thrilling an adventure a secret, but they'd agreed. The park officials wanted no publicity either. The only news mention of the incident was that a spook, which somehow had found its way from one of the northern wildlife preserves into Melna Park, had been killed there by a visitor's guard dog, and that the park was being carefully scanned to make sure no more of the dangerous animals had strayed in. Telzey's story to her friends was that there'd been a malfunction in the Cloudsplitter. The car had settled inertly to the ground, and when she got out to do something about it, the malfunction apparently cut out again, and the Cloudsplitter floated up out of her reach before she could stop it and drifted away. She'd started walking back to Cil Canyon, and presently found the spook on her trail. The Cloudsplitter was located by a police car next day, fifty miles beyond the park borders, and restored to its owner. Before leaving the park, Telzey quietly recovered Dunker's watch and the other articles Robane had made her discard at the house.

The only people who could see a connection between the dead spook and Robane were the smugglers who'd provided him with an animal of that kind, and they'd have no interest in the fact that it was dead. If anyone who might be associated with Robane in his general work with psi machines became aware of his present condition, the mental damage would be attributed to a miscalculated experiment. Psi machines were considered uncertain devices in that respect. In any case, there was nothing to link Telzey to him. Nor was there really any reason why she couldn't go quietly back to Melna Park at any time to conclude her investigation. She wouldn't need to come within half a mile of the house for that.

She kept putting it off. She wasn't quite sure why. When the weekend came around, she simply found herself unwilling to make the trip. Robane was unfinished business. It wasn't usually her way at all to leave unfinished business lying around. But she told herself she'd take care of it the following week.

One night then she had a dream. It was an uncomfortable, sweaty, nightmarish sort of dream, though nothing much really happened. It seemed to go on for some time. She appeared to be floating in the air near Robane's house, watching it from various angles, aware that Robane watched her in turn, hating her for what she'd done to him, and waiting for a chance to destroy her. In the dream, Telzey reminded herself quite reasonably that it wasn't possible—Robane couldn't remember what she'd done or anything about her; he wouldn't recognize her if she were standing before him. Then she realized suddenly that it wasn't Robane but the house itself which watched her with such spiteful malice, and that something was about to happen to her. She woke up with a start of fright.

That settled it. She lay awake a while, considering. A weekend was coming up again. She could fly to Melna Park after her last scheduled lecture in the afternoon, and register at a park hotel. She'd have two full days if necessary to wind up matters at Robane's house. That certainly would be time enough. She'd extract the remaining information she wanted from him, then see to it that somebody among the park authorities discovered a good reason to pay the recluse a visit at his home. When they saw the condition he was in, they'd transfer him to an institution; and Robane shouldn't be disturbing her sleep again.

He did, however, that night in her room at the park hotel. Or something did. She'd retired soon after dinner, wanting to get off to an early start, found then that she wasn't at all sleepy, tuned in somnomusic, switched on the window screen, and went over to it in the darkened room. She stood there a while, looking out. In the cluster light, Melna Park sloped away, dim and vast, toward the northern mountains. Robane's house lay behind a fold of the mountains. At the restricted pace possible in the park, it would take her almost four hours to get to the house from the hotel tomorrow—twice the time she'd spent crossing half a continent from Pehanron College in the evening.

The music was producing drowsiness in her, but tensions seemed to fight it. It was almost an hour before she got to bed and fell asleep, and it turned then into an uncomfortable night. There were periods of disagreeable dreaming, of which she could recall only scraps when she woke up. For the most part, she napped fitfully, kept coming awake. Something in her simply didn't want to relax; and as she began to go to sleep and her mental screens loosened normally, it drew them abruptly tight, bringing her back to weary alertness. She was up at daybreak at last, heavy-lidded and irritable. But a cold shower opened her eyes, and after she'd had breakfast, she seemed reasonably refreshed.

Ten minutes later, she was on her way to Robane's house through a breezy late-autumn morning. Melna Park was famed for varied and spectacular color changes in its vegetation as winter approached, and the tourist traffic was much heavier now than three weeks ago. Almost everywhere Telzey looked, aircars floated past, following the rolling contours of the ground. The Cloudsplitter moved along at the steady thirty miles an hour to which it was restricted. She'd slipped the canopy down; sun warmth seeped through her, while a chilled wind intermittently whipped her hair about her cheeks. Nighttime tensions grew vague and unreal. The relaxation which had eluded Telzey at the hotel came to her, and she was tempted to ground the car and settle down for an hour's nap in the sunshine before going on. But she wanted to reach the house early enough to be finished with Robane before evening.

Near noon, she reached the series of mile-wide plateaus dropping from the point where Cil Canyon cut through the mountains to the southern forests where Robane's house stood. She circled in toward the house, brought it presently into the car's viewscreen. It looked precisely as she remembered seeing it in the cluster light, neat, trim, quiet. A maintenance robot moved slowly about in the garden.

She considered relaxing her screens and directing a probing thought to Robane's mind from where she was. But she had most of the day left, and a remnant of uneasiness made her wary. She dropped the car behind a rise which hid Robane's house from her, moved on back of the rise for about a mile and settled to the ground at the edge of a stand of trees. Carrying a pocket telscreen, she walked to the top of the rise and across it, threading her way among the trees until she came to a point from where she could watch the house without being picked up in scanning devices from there.

She kept the house area in the telscreen for about ten minutes. The only sign of life was the tending machine in the garden. That was out of sight in some shrubbery for a while, then emerged and began moving back and forth across one of the lawns while a silvery mist arising from the shrubbery indicated a watering system had been turned on. Finally the robot trundled to the side of the house and paused before it. A wide door slid open in the wall, and the machine rolled inside.

Telzey put the telscreen down. She'd had a look through the door before it closed. A large aircar stood behind it. Robane, as was to be expected in his present state, should be at home.

And now, she decided, a light—a very light—probe. Just enough to make quite sure Robane was, in fact, as she'd left him, that there'd been no unforeseen developments of any kind around here.

Leaning against the sun-warm trunk of a tall tree, she closed her eyes and thinned the screens about her mind, let them open out. She felt a sudden tug of anxiety resistance, but the screens stayed open. The blended whispers of life currents about her began to flow into her awareness.

Everything seemed normal. She flicked a thread of thought down to the forest then, to Robane's house, touched for a moment the patterns she remembered.

Something like a shout flashed through her mind. Not words, nothing even partly verbalized; nevertheless, it was a clear sharp command, accompanied by a gust of hate like a curse. The hate was directed at her. The command—

In the split instant of shock as her screens contracted into a tight hard shield, she'd seemed aware of a blurred dark image rushing toward her. Then the image, the command-and-hate impressions, the touch of Robane's mind, were blocked off together by the shield.

Telzey opened her eyes, glanced about. For long seconds, she remained motionless. The trees stirred above as a breeze rustled past. Here in the world of material reality, nothing seemed changed or different. But what had she run into at Robane's house?

A sound reached her . . . the rolling thunder of explosion. It faded away, echoing across the plain.

It seemed to have come from the forest to the south. Telzey listened a moment, moved forward until she could look out from behind the trees.

An ugly rolling cloud of yellow smoke partly concealed the area where the house had stood. But it was clear that house and garden had been violently obliterated.

And that, Telzey thought numbly, was in part her answer.

By the time she got back to the Cloudsplitter and lifted it from the ground, tourist aircars were gliding in cautiously toward the site of the explosion. A ranger car screamed down out of the sky, passed above her and vanished. Telzey remained behind the rise and continued to move to the west. She was almost certain that whoever had blown up Robane in his house wasn't physically in the area. But there was no need to expose herself any more than she'd already done.

Robane had been used as bait—bait to trap a psi. The

fact that he'd been destroyed then indicated that whoever set the trap believed the psi for whom it was intended had been caught. And there must be a reason for that belief. In whatever she did now, she'd better be extremely careful.

She brought the thought impressions she'd recorded back into awareness, examined them closely.

They were brief but strong and vivid. She began to distinguish details she hadn't consciously noted in the instant of sensing them. This psi was human, must be; and yet the flavor of the thought forms suggested almost an alien species. They were heavy with arrogance as if the psi himself felt he was different from and superior to human beings. The thrust of hard power carrying the impressions had been as startling to her as the sudden angry roar of an animal nearby. She recalled feeling that a curse was being pronounced on her.

And blended in was a communication—not intended for her, and not too clear. It was, Telzey thought, the sort of mental shortcode which developed among associated telepaths: a flick of psi which might transmit an involved meaning. She could guess the basic meaning here. Success! The quarry was snared! He'd had one or more companions. His own kind, whatever it was.

Finally, the third part, the least clear section of the thought structure. It had death in it. Her death. It was a command; and she was almost certain it had been directed at the indistinct shape she'd seemed to glimpse rushing toward her. Something that might have been a large animal.

Her death . . . how? Telzey swallowed uncomfortably. They might have been involved with the ring which had catered to Robane's criminal inclinations—minds like that would have no objection to delivering one human being to another, to be hunted down and killed for sport. But psis would have recognized a special value in Robane. He was a precision instrument that could provide them with machines to extend and amplify their powers. His inventive genius had been at the disposal of a telepath who'd set him problems and left him to work them out, not knowing why he did it, or for whose benefit, in the solitude of Melna Park.

She'd put an end to Robane's usefulness and might presently have come on clues pointing to them in the unconscious recesses of his mind if they hadn't discovered what had been done. They knew it was the work of another psi. She'd sealed most of Robane's memories away but left them intact; and that told them she planned to return to look for more information. They could have destroyed Robane at once, but they wanted to dispose of the unidentified meddler. So they'd set up the trap with Robane's mind as the bait. The psi who touched that mind again would spring the trap. And, some twenty minutes ago, cautious and light as her touch had been, she'd sprung it.

Immediately afterwards, she'd locked her screens. In doing it, she might have escaped whatever was planned for her. But she had to accept the probability that she still was in the trap—and she didn't yet know what it was.

The Cloudsplitter went gliding at its thirty miles an hour across the upper plateaus of the plain, a hundred feet above the ground. The southern forest where the house had stood had sunk out of sight. The flanks of the mountains curved away ahead. Telzey turned the car in farther toward them. Another car slipped past at the edge of her vision, half a mile to the left. She had an impulse to follow it, to remain near other people. But she kept the Cloudsplitter on its course. The company of others would bring her no safety, and mingling with them might distract her attention dangerously.

She set the car on automatic control, sat gazing at the mountains through the windshield. The other impression at the moment of touching Robane's mind— the shape like an animal's—it might have been a hallucination, her own mind's symbol of some death energy directed at her. Psi could kill swiftly, could be used as a weapon by minds which understood its use for that purpose and could handle the forces they turned on another. But if that had been the trap, it seemed to her she would have interpreted it differently—not as a moving shadow, a half-glimpsed animal shape, an image darting toward her.

What else could it be? Telzey shook her head. She didn't know, and she couldn't guess. She could find out; eventually she'd have to find out. But not yet.

She glanced at the car clock. Give it another hour. Evidently they hadn't identified her physically; but it could do no harm to place more physical distance between herself and the area of Robane's house before she made any revealing moves. Mentally, she should have seemed to vanish for them as her shield closed. The difficulty was that the shield couldn't stay closed indefinitely.

7

An hour later, the effects of having passed a night with very little sleep were becoming noticeable. There were moments of reduced wakefulness and physical lassitude of which she'd grow suddenly aware. The nearest ranger car would have provided her with a stimulant if she'd put out a communicator call for one, but her enemies might have means of monitoring events in the park she didn't know about. It didn't seem at all advisable to draw attention to herself in that way, or in any other way. She'd simply have to remain alert long enough to get this situation worked out.

The test she intended was a simple one. The psi shield would flash open, instantly be closed again. During that moment, her perceptions, fully extended, would be set to receive two impressions: thought patterns of the telepath who'd laid a trap for her, and the animal shape involved with the trap. If either was still in her mental vicinity, some trace would be obtained, however faintly. If neither was there, she could begin to believe she'd eluded them. Not indefinitely; psis could determine who had destroyed Robane's effectiveness if they put in enough work on it. But that would be another problem. Unless they were as intently prepared as she was to detect some sign from her now, the momentary exposure of her mind should pass unnoticed.

The shield flicked open, flicked shut, as her sensitized perceptions made their recording. Telzey sat still for a moment then, feeling the heavy drumming of fear.

Slowly, like an afterimage, she let the recorded picture form again in awareness.

A dark beast shape. What kind of beast she didn't know. Something like a great uncouth baboon—a big heavy head, strong body supported on four huge hand-paws.

As the shield opened, she had the feeling of seeing it near her, three-dimensional, every detail clearly etched though it stood in a vague nothingness. The small red eyes stared in her direction. And short as the moment of exposure was, she was certain she'd seen it start in recognition, begin moving toward her, before it vanished beyond the shield again.

What was it? A projection insinuated into her mind by the other telepath in the instant of contact between them —something she was supposed to develop to her own destruction now?

She didn't think so. It seemed too real, too alertly, menacingly, alive. In some way she'd seen what was there—the vague animal shape she'd glimpsed—nearby and no longer vague. In physical space, it might be hundreds of miles away; or perhaps it was nowhere in that sense at present. In the other reality they shared, she hadn't drawn away from it. After its attention was turned on her, it had waited while she was concealed by her shield, moved closer at the brief new impression it received of her mind. . . . What would happen when, in its manner, it reached her, touched her?

She didn't know the answer to that. She let the image fade, began searching for traces of the telepathic mind associated with it. After long seconds, she knew nothing

58

had been recorded in her perceptions there. The psi was gone. He'd prepared the trap, set the creature on her, then apparently turned away—as if confident he'd done all that needed to be done to dispose of her.

The thought was briefly more chilling than the waiting beast image. But if it was only an animal she had to deal with, Telzey told herself, escape might be an easier matter than it would have been if minds like the one she had encountered had remained on her trail.

The animal still seemed bad enough. She'd never heard of a creature which tracked down prey by sensing mental emanations, as this one evidently did. It might be a native of some unrecorded world, brought to the Hub for the specific purpose of turning it into a hunter of human psis—psis who could make trouble for its masters. It knew about mind shields. Either it had dealt with such defenses in its natural state, or it had been trained to handle them. At any rate, it seemed quite aware that it need only wait with a predator's alert patience until the quarry's shield relaxed. As hers would eventually. She couldn't stay awake indefinitely; and asleep she didn't have enough control to keep so steady and relentless a watcher from detecting mental activity.

It had been a trap in several ways then. If she'd entered Robane's house, she would have vanished in the explosion with him. Since she'd checked first, they'd turned this thing on her. It was either to destroy her outright or force her into behavior that would identify her to its masters—and she had to get rid of it before the need to sleep brought down her defenses.

She felt the psi bolt begin to assemble itself. No ordinary brief sharp slash of psi was likely to serve here. She'd turn the heaviest torrent of energy she could channel on her uncanny pursuer. Something like a black electric swirling about her was sending ripples over her skin.

Not at all a pleasant sensation, but she let it develop. It would be to her disadvantage to wait any longer; and since the psis weren't around themselves, this was as good a place as any for the encounter. The Cloudsplitter was drifting up a wide valley into the higher ranges of the park. There was a chill in the breeze and few tourists about. At the moment she saw only three aircars, far ahead.

The energy pattern grew denser, became a shuddering thunder. She gathered it in, held it aimed like a gun, let it build up until she was trembling almost unbearably with its violence, then abruptly released her shield.

Almost at once, seeing the dark shape plunge at her through the nothing-space of psi, she knew that on this beast it wasn't going to work. Energy smashed about it but found no entry point; it wasn't being touched. She expended the bolt's fury as the shape rushed up, snapped the shield shut before it reached her—immediately found herself slewing the Cloudsplitter around in a sharp turn as if to avoid a physical collision. There was a sound then, a deep bubbling howl, which chilled her through and through.

Glancing around, she saw it for an instant twenty feet behind the car—no mind image, but a thick powerful animal body, plunging head downward, stretched out as if it were diving, through the air of Melna Park. Then it vanished.

It was a psi creature whose natural prey were other psi creatures, she thought; that was why she hadn't been able to touch it. Its species had a developed immunity to such defensive blasts and could ignore them. It had a sense through which it traced out and approached the minds of prospective victims, and it had the psi ability to flick itself across space when it knew by the mind contact where they were to be found. For the kill it needed

60

only physical weapons—the strength of its massive body, its great teeth and the broad flat nails of the reaching beast hands which had seemed only inches from her when the shield shut them from view. If she hadn't swerved aside in that instant, the thing would have crashed down into the car and torn the life out of her moments later.

Her attempt to confront it had made the situation more immediately dangerous. Handling that flood of deadly energy had drained her strength; and a kind of dullness was settling on her now, composed in part of growing fatigue and in part of a puzzled wonder that she really seemed able to do nothing to get away from the thing. It was some minutes before she could push the feeling aside and get her thoughts again into some kind of order.

The creature's dip through space seemed to have confused it temporarily; at any rate, it had lost too much contact with her to materialize near her again, though she didn't doubt it was still very close mentally. There were moments when she thought she could sense its presence just beyond the shield. She'd had a respite, but no more than that. It probably wasn't even a very intelligent animal; a species with its abilities and strength wouldn't need much mental equipment to get along in its world. But she was caught in a game which was being played by the animal's rules, not hers, and there still seemed no way to get around them.

Some time past the middle of the afternoon, she edged the Cloudsplitter down into a cluster of thickets on sloping ground, brushing through the vegetation until the car was completely concealed. She shut off its engines and climbed out, stood swaying unsteadily for a moment, then turned and pushed her way out of the thickets.

If she'd remained sitting in the car, she would have been asleep in minutes. By staying on her feet, she might gain another period of time to work out the solution. But she wasn't far from the point where she'd have to call the park rangers and ask them to get a fix on her and come to her help. Stimulants could keep her awake for several days.

At that point, she would have invited danger from a new source. A public appeal for help from someone in Melna Park could be a beacon to her enemies; she had to count on the possibility that they waited alertly for just such an indication that their hunter had the quarry pinned down. She might be identified very quickly then.

But to try to stay awake on her own for even another fifteen or twenty minutes could be fatal. The thing was *near!* A dozen times she'd been on the verge of drifting into a half-dreaming level where outside reality and the universe of psi seemed to blend, and had been jolted awake by a suddenly growing sense of the psi beast's presence.

Getting out of the car and on her feet had roused her a little. The cold of the mountain air produced a further stimulating effect. She'd come far up into a region of the park which already seemed touched by winter. It might have been almost half an hour since she'd last seen a tourist car or any other indication of humanity on the planet.

She stood looking around, rubbing her arms with her hands to warm them. She was above a rounded dip in the mountains between two adjoining ridges. Hip-high brown grass and straggling trees filled the dip. A swift narrow stream wound through it. She'd grounded the car three quarters of the way up the western side. The far side was an almost vertical rock wall, festooned with yellow cobwebs of withering vines. That half of the dip was still bathed in sunlight coming over the top of the ridge behind her. Her side was in shadow.

She shivered in the chill, shook her head to drive away another wave of drowsiness. She seemed unable to concentrate on the problem of the psi beast. Her thoughts shifted to the sun-warmed rocks she'd crossed at the top of the ridge as she turned the Cloudsplitter down into the little valley.

She pictured herself sitting there, warmed by the sun. It was a convincing picture. In imagination she felt the sun on her shoulders and back, the warm rock beneath her, saw the dry thorny fall growth about—

Her eyes flickered, widened thoughtfully. After a moment, she brought the picture back into her mind.

I'm here, she thought. I'm sitting in the sun. I'm half asleep, nodding, feeling the warmth—forgetting I'm in danger. The wind blows over the rocks, and the bushes are rustling all around me. . . .

She relaxed the shield—"I'm here, Bozo!"—closed it.

She stood in the shadow of the western ridge, shivering and chilled, listening. Far above, for a moment, there'd been noises as if something plunged heavily about in the growth at the top of the ridge. Then the noises ended abruptly.

Telzey's gaze shifted down into the dip between the ridges, followed the course of the little stream up out of the shadows to a point where it ran between flat sandy banks, glittering and sparkling in the afternoon sun— held there.

And now I'm *here,* she thought, and nodded down at the little stream. I'm sitting in warm sand, in the sun again, sheltered from the wind, listening to the friendly water—

The shield opened. For an instant.

"I'm here!"

Looking down from the shaded slope, shield sealed tight, she saw, for the second time that day, Bozo the beast appear in Melna Park, half in the stream, half out. Its heavy head swung this way and that; it leaped forward, wheeled, glared about, plunged suddenly out of sight among the trees. For an instant, she heard its odd howling voice, like amplified drunken human laughter, furious with frustrated eagerness.

Telzey leaned back against the tree behind her, closed her eyes. Drowsiness rolled in immediately in sweet heavy treacherous waves. She shook her head, drove it back.

Darkness, she thought. Darkness, black and cold. . . . Black, black all around me—because I've fallen asleep, Bozo! Now you can get me—

Blackness closed in on her mind like a rush of wind. The shield slipped open.

"Bozo! I'm HERE!"

In the blackness, Bozo's image flashed up before her, jaws wide, red eyes blazing, great arms sweeping out to seize her.

The shield snapped shut.

Eyes still closed, Telzey swayed against the tree, listening to the echoes of the second explosion she'd heard today. This one had been short and sharp, monstrously loud, like a thunderbolt slamming into the earth a hundred feet from her.

She shook her head, opened her eyes, looked across the dip. The cliff face on the eastern side had changed its appearance. A jagged dark fissure showed in it, beginning at the top, extending halfway down to the valley. Puffs of mineral dust still drifted out of the fissure into the open air.

She'd wondered what would happen if something more than five hundred pounds of solid animal materialized suddenly deep inside solid rock. She'd expected it might be something like this. This time, Bozo hadn't been able to flick back into no-space again.

"Good-by, Bozo!" she said aloud, across the dip. "I won't miss you at all!"

That had been one part of it, she thought.

And now the other. . . .

The shield thinned again, opened out. And stayed open—one minute, two minutes, three—as her perceptions spread, searching for impressions of the psi mind that had cursed her with Bozo, long, long hours ago, at Robane's house. That mind, or any mind like it.

And there was nothing. Nowhere around here, for many miles at least, was anyone thinking of her at the moment, giving her any attention at all.

Then you've lost me for now, she told them. She turned, stumbling, her balance not too good at the moment on the rocky ground, and pushed back through the bushes to the point where she'd left the Cloudsplitter. A minute later, she'd lifted the car above the ridges, swung it around to the south. Its canopy was closed and she was luxuriously soaking in the warmth of the heaters. She wanted to go to sleep very badly now, but there was one thing still to be done. It was nearly finished.

One section, a tiny section, of her mind was forming itself into an alarm system. It would remain permanently on guard against psis of the kind who'd nearly trapped her for good. At the slightest, most distant indication that minds like that were about, long before she became consciously aware of them, her screens would lock into a shield and she would know why.

It was necessary. There was no reason to believe she was done with them. They'd relied on their trap; and it had failed. But they could go back now to the night Robane's spook had been killed and try to find out who'd been involved in that. She'd covered herself as well as she could. It would involve a great deal of probing around in the minds of park personnel, a detailed checking of visitors' registers at the entrance stations; but eventually they could work out a line on the psi who'd trespassed on their operation and locate her. If she were doing it herself, it shouldn't take more than two weeks. She had to assume it would take them no longer.

Telzey felt her new alarm system complete itself, reached over and set the Cloudsplitter on the automatic controls which would guide it back down through the mountains into the warm southern plains of Melna Park to drift along with other tourist cars. Later, she thought, she'd decide what she'd have to be doing about the psis within the next two weeks. Later—

She slumped back gently in the seat and was instantly asleep.

8

Telzey was about to sit down for a snack in her bungalow before evening classes when the ring she'd worn on her left forefinger for the past week gave her a sting.

It was a fairly emphatic sting. Emphatic enough to have brought her out of a sound sleep if she'd happened to be sleeping. She grimaced, pulled off the ring, rubbed her finger, slipped the ring back on, went to the Com-Web and tapped a button.

Elsewhere on the grounds of Pehanron College several other ComWebs started burring a special signal. One or the other of them would now be switched on, and somebody would listen to what she had to say. She'd become used to that; the realization didn't disturb her.

What she said to her course computer was, "This is Telzey Amberdon. Cancel me for both classes tonight."

The computer acknowledged. Winter rains had been pounding against Pehanron's weather shields throughout the day. Telzey got into boots, long coat and gloves, wrapped a scarf around her head, and went out to the carport at the back of the bungalow. A few minutes later, her car slid out of Pehanron's main gate, switched on its fog beams and arrowed up into a howling storm.

Somebody would be following her through the dark sky. She'd got used to that, too.

She went into a public ComWeb booth not long after leaving the college and dialed a number. The screen lit up and a face appeared.

"Hello, Klayung," she said. "I got your signal. I'm calling from Beale."

"I know," said Klayung. He was an executive of the Psychology Service, old, stringy, mild-mannered. "Leave the booth, turn left, walk down to the corner. There's a car waiting."

"All right," Telzey said. "Anything else?"

"Not till I see you."

It was raining as hard on Beale as on Pehanron, and this section of the town had no weather shielding. Head bent, Telzey ran down the street to the corner. The door to the back compartment of a big aircar standing there opened as she came up. She slipped inside. The door closed.

Clouds blotted out the lights of Beale below as she was fishing tissues from her purse to dry her face. The big car was a space job though it didn't look like one. She could see the driver silhouetted beyond the partition. They were alone in the car.

She directed a mental tap at the driver, touched a mind shield, standard Psychology Service type. There was no flicker of response or recognition, so he was no psi operator.

Telzey settled back on the seat. Life had become a rather complicated business these days. She'd reported her experiences in Melna Park to the Psychology Service, which, among other things, handled problems connected with psi and did it quietly to avoid disturbing the public. The Service people went to work on the information she could give them. While she waited for results from that quarter, she had some matters to take care of herself.

Until now, her psi armament had seemed adequate. She should be able to wind up her law studies at Pehanron in another year, and she'd intended to wait till then before giving serious attention to psi and what could be done with it—or, at any rate, to what she could do with it. Clearly, that idea had better be dropped at once! Half a psi talent could turn into a dangerous gift when it drew the attention of others who didn't stick to halfway measures. She'd made a few modifications immediately. When she locked her screens into a shield now, they stayed locked without further attention, whether she was drowsy, wide awake or sound asleep, until she decided to open them again. *That* particular problem wouldn't recur! What she needed, however, was a general crash course in dealing with unfriendly mentalities of more than average capability. The Service might be willing to train her, but not necessarily along the lines she wanted. Besides, she preferred not to become too obligated to them.

There was a psi she knew, an independent like herself, who should have the required experience, if she could get him to share it. Sams Larking wasn't exactly a friend. He was, in fact, untrustworthy, unethical, underhanded and sneaky. The point nevertheless was that he was psi-sneaky in a highly accomplished manner, and packed a heavy mind clout. Telzey looked him up.

"Why should I help make you any tougher than you are?" Sams inquired.

She explained that Service operators had been giving her too much attention lately. She didn't like the idea of having somebody prying around her like that.

Sams grunted. He hated the Psychology Service.

"Been up to something they don't approve of, eh?" he said. "All right. Let's see if we can't have a few surprises ready for them the next time. You want to be able to spot them without letting them spot you, or send them home with lumps—that kind of thing?"

"That kind of thing," Telzey agreed. "I particularly want to learn how to work through my own screens. I've noticed you're very good at that. . . . The lumps could be sort of permanent, too!"

Sams looked briefly startled. "Getting rather ferocious, aren't you?" He studied her. "Well, we'll see how much you can handle. It can't be done in an hour or two, you know. Drop in at the ranch first thing this weekend, and we'll give it a couple of days. The house is psi-blocked, in case somebody comes snooping."

He added, "I'll behave. Word of honor! This will be business—if I can sharpen you up enough, you might be useful to me someday. Get a good night's rest before you come. I'll work you till you're begging to quit."

Work her relentlessly he did. Telzey didn't ask for time out. She was being drilled through techniques it might have taken her months to develop by herself. They discovered she could handle them. Then something went wrong.

She didn't know immediately what it was. She looked over at Sams.

He was smiling, a bit unpleasantly.

"Controlled, aren't you?"

Telzey felt a touch of apprehension. She considered. "Yes," she said, "I am. I must be! But—"

She hesitated. Sams nodded.

"You've been under control for the past half-hour. You wouldn't know it now if I hadn't let you know it—

and you still don't understand how it's being done, so there's nothing you can do about it, is there?" He grinned suddenly, and Telzey felt the psi controls she hadn't been able to sense till then release her.

"Just a demonstration, this time!" Sams said. "Don't let yourself get caught again. Get a few hours' sleep, and we'll go on. You're a good student."

Around the middle of the second day, he said, "You've done fine! There really isn't much more I can do for you. But now a special gimmick. I never expected to show it to anyone, but let's see if you can work it. It takes plenty of coordination. Screens tight, both sides. You scan. If I spot you, you get jolted so hard your teeth rattle!"

After a few seconds, she said, "I'm there."

Sams nodded.

"Good! I can't tell it. Now I'll leave you an opening, just a flash. You're to try to catch it and slam me at the same instant."

"Well, wait a moment!" Telzey said. "Supposing I don't just try—I *do* it?"

"Don't worry. I'll block. Watch out for the counter!"

Sams's screen opening flicked through her awareness five seconds later. She slammed. But, squeamishly perhaps, she held back somewhat on the bolt.

It took her an hour to bring Sams around. He sat up groggily at last.

"How do you feel?" she asked.

He shook his head. "Never mind. Good-by! Go home. You've graduated. I'm a little sorry for the Service."

Telzey knew she hadn't given the Service much to work on, but there were a few possible lines of general investigation. Since the Melna Park psis apparently had set Robane the task of developing psi machines for them, they should be interested in psi machines generally. They might, or might not, be connected with the criminal ring with which he'd had contacts; if they were, they presumably controlled it. And, of course, they definitely did make use of a teleporting creature, of which there seemed to be no record otherwise, to kill people.

She'd been able to add one other thing about them which could be significant. They might be a mutant strain of humanity. The impressions of the thought forms she'd retained seemed to have a distinctive quality she'd never sensed in human minds before.

A machine copied the impressions from her memory. They were analyzed, checked against Service files. They did have a distinctive quality, and it was one which wasn't on record. Special investigators with back-up teams began to scan Orado systematically, trying to pick up mental traces which might match the impressions, while outfits involved in psi technology, along with assorted criminal organizations, were scrutinized for indications of telepathic control. Neither approach produced results.

The Service went on giving Orado primary attention but extended its investigations next to the Hub worlds in general. There the sheer size of the Hub's populations raised immense difficulties. Psi machines were regarded by many as a coming thing; on a thousand worlds, great numbers of people currently were trying to develop effective designs. Another multitude, of course, was involved in organized crime. Eccentric forms of murder, including a variety which conceivably could have been carried out by Telzey's psi beasts, were hardly uncommon. Against such a background, the secretive psis might remain invisible indefinitely.

"Nevertheless," Klayung, who was in charge of the

Service operation, told Telzey, "we may be getting a pattern! It's not too substantial, but it's consistent. If it indicates what it seems to, the people you became involved with are neither a local group nor a small one. In fact, they appear to be distributed rather evenly about the more heavily populated Federation worlds."

She didn't like that. "What kind of pattern is it?"

"Violent death, without witnesses and of recurring specific types—types which could be explained by your teleporting animal. The beast kills but not in obvious beast manner. It remains under restraint. If, for example, it had been able to reach you in Melna Park, it might have broken your neck, dropped you out of your aircar, and vanished. Elsewhere it might have smothered or strangled you, suggesting a human assailant. There are a number of variations repetitive enough to be included in the pattern. We're trying to establish connections among the victims. So far we don't have any. You remain our best lead."

Telzey already had concluded that. There were no detectable signs, but she was closely watched, carefully guarded. If another creature like Bozo the Beast should materialize suddenly in her college bungalow while she was alone, it would be dead before it touched her. That was reassuring at present. But it didn't solve the problem.

Evidence that the psis had found her developed within ten days. As Klayung described it, there was now a new kind of awareness of Telzey about Pehanron College, of her coming and going. Not among friends and acquaintances but among people she barely knew by sight, who, between them, were in a good position to tell approximately where she was, what she did, much of the time. Then there was the matter of ComWebs. No attempt had been made to tamper with the instrument in her bungalow. But a number of other ComWebs responded whenever it was switched on; and her conversations were monitored.

"These people aren't controlled in the ordinary sense," Klayung remarked. "They've been given a very few specific instructions, carry them out, and don't know they're doing it. They have no conscious interest in you. And they haven't been touched in any other way. All have wide-open minds. Somebody presumably scans those minds periodically for information. He hasn't been caught at it. Whoever arranged this is a highly skilled operator. It's an interesting contrast to that first, rather crude, trap prepared for you."

"That one nearly worked," Telzey said thoughtfully. "Nobody's tried to probe me here—I've been waiting for it. They know who I am, and they must be pretty sure I'm the one who did away with Bozo. You think they suspect I'm being watched?"

"I'd suspect it in their place," Klayung said. "They know who you are—not what you are. Possibly a highly talented junior Service operator. We're covered, I think. But I'd smell a trap. We have to assume that whoever is handling the matter on their side also smells a trap."

"Then what's going to happen?"

Klayung shrugged.

"I know it isn't pleasant, Telzey, but it's a waiting game here—unless they make a move. They may not do it. They may simply fade away again."

She made a small grimace. "That's what I'm afraid of."

"I know. But we're working on other approaches. They've been able to keep out of our way so far. But we're aware of them now—we'll be watching for slips, and sooner or later we'll pick up a line to them."

Sooner or later! She didn't like it at all! She'd become

a pawn. A well-protected one—but one with no scrap of privacy left, under scrutiny from two directions. She didn't blame Klayung or the Service. For them, this was one problem among very many they had to handle, always short of sufficiently skilled personnel, always trying to recruit any psi of the slightest usable ability who was willing to be recruited. She was one of those who hadn't been willing, not wanting the restrictions it would place on her. She couldn't complain.

But she couldn't accept the situation either. It had to be resolved.

Somehow. . . .

9

"What do you know about Tinokti?" Klayung asked.

"Tinokti?" Telzey had been transferred from the car that picked her up in Beale to a small space cruiser standing off Orado. She, Klayung, and the car driver seemed to be the only people aboard. "I haven't been there, and I haven't made a special study of it." She reflected. "Nineteen hours liner time from Orado. Rather dense population. High living standards. World-wide portal circuit system—the most involved in the Federation. A social caste system that's also pretty involved. Government by syndicate—a scientific body, the Tongi Phon. Corrupt, but they have plenty of popular support. As scientists they're supposed to be outstanding in a number of fields." She shrugged. "That's it, mainly. Is it enough?"

Klayung nodded. "For now. I'll fill you in. The Tongi Phon's not partial to the Service. They've been working hard at developing a psi technology of their own. They've got farther than most, but still not very far. Their approach is much too conservative—paradoxes disturb them. But they've learned enough to be aware of a number of possibilities. That's made them suspicious of us."

"Well, they might have a good deal to hide," Telzey said.

"Definitely. They do what they can to limit our activities. A majority of the commercial and private circuits are psi-blocked, as a result of a carefully underplayed campaign of psi and psi machine scares. The Tongi Phon Institute is blocked, of course; the Phons wear mind shields. Tinokti in general presents extraordinary operational difficulties. So it was something of a surprise when we got a request for help today from the Tongi Phon."

"Help in what?" Telzey asked.

"Four high-ranking Phons," Klayung explained, "were found dead together in a locked and guarded vault area at the Institute. Their necks had been broken and the backs of the skulls caved in—in each case apparently by a single violent blow. The bodies showed bruises but no other significant damage."

She said after a moment, "Did the Institute find out anything?"

"Yes. The investigators assumed at first a temporary portal had been set up secretly to the vault. But there should have been residual portal energy detectable, and there wasn't. They did establish then that a life form of unknown type had been present at the time of the killings. Estimated body weight close to ten hundred pounds."

Telzey nodded. "That was one of Bozo's relatives, all right!"

"We can assume it. The vault area was psi-blocked. So that's no obstacle to them. The Phons are badly frightened. Political assassinations are no novelty at the Institute, but here all factions lost leading members. Nobody feels safe. They don't know the source of the threat or the reason for it, but they've decided psi may have been involved. Within limits, they're willing to cooperate with the Service."

He added, "As it happens, we'd already been giving Tinokti special attention. It's one of perhaps a dozen Hub worlds where a secret psi organization would find almost ideal conditions. Since they've demonstrated an interest in psi machines, the Institute's intensive work in the area should be a further attraction. Mind shields or not, it wouldn't be surprising to discover the psis have been following that project for some time. So the Service will move to Tinokti in strength. If we can trap a sizable nest, it might be a long step toward rounding up the lot wherever they're hiding."

He regarded Telzey a moment.

"Because of its nature," he remarked, "this isn't technically even a classified operation. It's one that has no official existence. It isn't happening. After it's over with, it won't have happened."

Telzey said, "You've told me because you want me to go to Tinokti?"

"Yes. We should be able to make very good use of you. The fact that you're sensitized to the psis' mind type gives you an advantage over our operators. And your sudden interest in Tinokti after what's occurred might stimulate some reaction from the local group."

"I'll be bait?" Telzey said.

"In part. Our moment to moment tactics will depend on developments, of course."

She nodded. "Well, I'm bait here, and I want them off my neck. What will the arrangement be?"

"You're making the arrangement," Klayung told her. "A psi arrangement, to keep you in character—the junior Service operator who's maintaining her well-established cover as a law student. You'll have Pehanron assign you to a field trip to Tinokti to do a paper on the legalistic aspects of the Tongi Phon government."

"It'll have to be cleared with the Institute," Telzey said.

"We'll take care of that."

"All right." She considered. "I may have to work on three or four minds. When do I leave?"

"A week from today."

Telzey nodded. "That's no problem then. There's one thing. . . ."

"Yes?"

"The psis have been so careful not to give themselves away here. Why should they create an obvious mystery on Tinokti?"

Klayung said, "I'm wondering. There may be something the Phons haven't told us. However, the supposition at present is that the beast failed to follow its instructions exactly—as the creatures may, in fact, have done on other occasions with less revealing results. You had the impression that Bozo wasn't too intelligent."

"Yes, I did," Telzey said. "But it doesn't seem very intelligent either to use an animal like that where something could go seriously wrong, as it certainly might in a place like the Institute. Particularly when they still haven't found out what happened to their other psi beast on Orado."

What were they?

Telzey had fed questions to information centers. Reports about psi mutant strains weren't uncommon, but one had to go a long way back to find something like confirming evidence. She condensed the information she obtained, gave it, combined with her own recent experiences, to Pehanron's probability computer to digest.

The machine stated that she was dealing with descendants of the historical mind masters of Nalakia, the Elaigar.

She mentioned it to Klayung. He wasn't surprised. The Service's probability computers concurred.

"But that's impossible!" Telzey said, startled. The information centers had provided her with a great deal of material on the Elaigar. "If the records are right, they averaged out at more than five hundred pounds. Besides, they looked like ogres! How could someone like that be moving around in a Hub city without being noticed?"

Klayung said they wouldn't necessarily have to let themselves be seen, at least not by people who could talk about them. If they'd returned to the Hub from some other galactic section, they might have set up bases on unused nonoxygen worlds a few hours from their points of operation, almost safe from detection so long as their presence wasn't suspected. He wasn't discounting the possibility.

Telzey, going over the material again later, found that she didn't much care for the possibility. The Elaigar belonged to the Hub's early colonial period. They'd been physical giants with psi minds, a biostructure believed to be of human origin, developed by a science-based cult called the Grisands, which had moved out from the Old Territory not long before and established itself in a stronghold on Nalakia. In the Grisand idiom, Elaigar meant the Lion People. It suggested what the Grisands intended to achieve—a controlled formidable strain through which they could dominate the other humans on Nalakia and on neighboring colony worlds. But they lost command of their creation. The Elaigar turned on them, and the Grisands died in the ruins of their stronghold. Then the Elaigar set out on conquests of their own.

Apparently they'd been the terrors of that area of space for a number of years, taking over one colony after another. The humans they met and didn't kill were mentally enslaved and thereafter lived to serve them. Eventually, war fleets were assembled in other parts of the Hub; and the prowess of the Elaigar proved to be no match for superior space firepower. The survivors among them fled in ships crewed by their slaves and hadn't been heard from again.

Visual reproductions of a few of the slain mutants were included in the data Telzey had gathered. There hadn't been many available. The Hub's War Centuries lay between that time and her own; most of the colonial period's records had been destroyed or lost. Even dead and seen in the faded recordings, the Elaigar appeared as alarming as their reputation had been. There were a variety of giant strains in the Hub, but most of them looked reasonably human. The Elaigar seemed a different species. The massive bodies were like those of powerful animals, and the broad hairless faces brought to mind the faces of great cats.

But human the prototype must have been, Telzey thought—if it *was* Elaigar she'd met briefly on the psi level in Orado's Melna Park. The basic human mental patterns were discernible in the thought forms she'd registered. What was different might fit these images of the Nalakian mind masters and their brief, bloody Hub history. Klayung could be right.

"Well, just be sure," Jessamine Amberdon commented when Telzey informed her parents by ComWeb one evening that she'd be off on a field assignment to Tinokti next day, "that you're back ten days from now."

"Why?" asked Telzey.

"For the celebration, of course."

"Eh?"

Jessamine sighed. "Oh, Telzey. You've become the most absent-minded dear lately! That's your birthday, remember? You'll be sixteen."

10

Citizens of Tinokti tended to regard the megacities of other Federation worlds as overgrown primitive villages. They, or some seventy per cent of them, lived and worked in the enclosed portal systems called circuits. For most it was a comfortable existence; for many a luxurious one.

A portal, for practical purposes, was two points in space clamped together to form one. It was a method of moving in a step from here to there, within a limited but considerable range. Portal circuits could be found on many Hub worlds. On Tinokti they were everywhere. Varying widely in extent and complexity, serving many purposes, they formed the framework of the planet's culture.

On disembarking at the spaceport, Telzey had checked in at a great commercial circuit called the Luerral Hotel. It had been selected for her because it was free of the psi blocks in rather general use here otherwise. The Luerral catered to the interstellar trade; and the force patterns which created the blocks were likely to give people unaccustomed to them a mildly oppressive feeling of being enclosed. For Telzey's purpose, of course, they were more serious obstacles.

While registering, she was equipped with a guest key. The Luerral Hotel was exclusive; its portals passed only those who carried a Luerral key or were in the immediate company of somebody who did. The keys were accessories of the Luerral's central computer and on request gave verbal directions and other information. The one Telzey selected had the form of a slender ring. She let it guide her to her room, found her luggage had preceded her there, and made a call to the Tongi Phon Institute. Tinokti ran on Institute time; the official workday wouldn't begin for another three hours. But she was connected with someone who knew of her application to do legal research, and was told a guide would come to take her to the Institute when it opened.

She set out then on a stroll about the hotel and circled Tinokti twice in an hour's unhurried walk, passing through portals which might open on shopping malls, tropical parks or snowy mountain resorts, as the circuit dipped in and out of the more attractive parts of the planet. She was already at work for Klayung, playing the role of a psi operator who was playing the role of an innocent student tourist. She wore a tracer which pinpointed her for a net of spacecraft deployed about the planet. The bracelet on her left wrist was a Service communicator; and she was in wispy but uninterrupted mind contact with a Service telepath whose specialty it was to keep such contacts undetectable for other minds. She also had armed company unobtrusively preceding and following her. They were probing Tinokti carefully in many ways; she was now one of the probes. Her thoughts searched through each circuit section and the open areas surrounding it as she moved along. She picked up no conscious impressions of the Service's quarry. But twice during that hour's walk, the screens enclosing her mind like a flexing bubble tightened abruptly into a solid shield. Her automatic detectors, more sensitive than conscious probes, had responded to a passing touch of the type of mental patterns they'd been designed to warn her against. The psis were here—and evidently less cautious than they'd been on Orado after her first encounter with them.

When she'd come back to the hotel's Great Lobby, Gudast, her Service contact, inquired mentally, "Mind doing a little more walking?"

Telzey checked her watch. "Just so I'm not late for the Phons."

"We'll get you back in time."

"All right. Where do I go?"

Gudast said, "Those mind touches you reported came at points where the Luerral Hotel passes through major city complexes. We'd like you to go back to them, leave the circuit and see if you can pick up something outside."

She got short cut directions from the Luerral computer, set out again. The larger sections had assorted transportation aids, but, on the whole, circuit dwellers seemed to do a healthy amount of walking. Almost all of the traffic she saw was pedestrian.

She took an exit presently, found herself in one of the city complexes mentioned by Gudast. Her Luerral ring key informed her the hotel had turned her over to the guidance of an area computer and that the key remained at her service if she needed information. Directed by Gudast, she took a seat on a slideway, let it carry her along a main street. Superficially, the appearance of things here was not unlike that of some large city on Orado. The differences were functional. Psi blocks were all about, sensed as a gradually shifting pattern of barriers to probes as the slideway moved on with her. Probably less than a fifth of the space of the great buildings was locally open; everything else was taken up by circuit sections connected to other points of the planet, ranging in size from a few residential or storage rooms to several building levels. Milkily gleaming horizontal streaks along the sides of the buildings showed that many of the sections were protected by force fields. Tinokti's citizens placed a high value on privacy.

Telzey stiffened suddenly. "Defense reaction!" she told Gudast.

"Caught it," his thought whispered.

"It's continuing." She passed her tongue over her lips.

"See a good place to get off the slideway?"

Telzey glanced along the street, stood up. "Yes! Big display windows just ahead. Quite a few people."

"Sounds right."

She stepped off the slideway as it came up to the window fronts, walked over, started along the gleaming windows, then stopped, looking in at the displayed merchandise. "I'm there," she told Gudast. "Reaction stopped a moment ago."

"See what you can do. We're set up."

Her psi sensors reached out. She brought up the thought patterns she'd recorded in Melna Park and stored in memory, blurred them, projected them briefly —something carelessly let slip from an otherwise guarded mind. She waited.

Her screens tried to tighten again. She kept them as they were, overriding the automatic reaction. The something moved faintly into awareness—mind behind shielding, alert, questioning, perhaps suspicious. Still barely discernible.

"Easy—easy!" whispered Gudast. "I'm getting it. We're getting it. Don't push at all! Give us fifteen seconds—ten—"

Psi block!

The impression had vanished.

Somewhere the being producing it had moved into a psi-blocked section of this city complex. Perhaps deliberately, choosing mental concealment. Perhaps simply because that was where it happened to be going when its attention was caught for a moment by Telzey's broadcast pattern. The impression hadn't been sufficiently strong to say anything about it except that this had been a mind of the type Telzey had encountered on Orado. They'd all caught for an instant the specific qualities she'd recorded.

The instant hadn't been enough. Klayung had brought a number of living psi compasses to Tinokti operators who could have pinpointed the position of the body housing that elusive mentality, given a few more seconds in which to work.

They hadn't been given those seconds, and the mentality wasn't contacted again. Telzey went on presently to the other place where she'd sensed a sudden warning, and prowled about here and there outside the Luerral Circuit, while Klayung's pack waited for renewed indications. This time they drew a blank.

But it had been confirmed that the psis—some of them—were on Tinokti.

The problem would be how to dig them out of the planet-wide maze of force-screened and psi-blocked circuit sections.

Telzey's Institute guide, a young man named Phon Hajugan, appeared punctually with the beginning of Tinokti's workday. He informed Telzey he held the lowest Tongi Phon rank. The lower echelons evidently hadn't been informed of the recent killings in the Institute vault and their superiors' apprehensions—Phon

Hajugan was in a cheery and talkative mood. Telzey's probe disclosed that he was equipped with a chemical mind shield.

There was no portal connection between the Luerral Hotel's circuit and that of the Institute. Telzey and her guide walked along a block of what appeared to be a sizable residential town before reaching an entry portal of the Tongi Phon Circuit, where she was provided with another portal key. She'd been making note of the route; in future she didn't intend to be distracted by the presence of a guide. The office to which Phon Hajugan conducted her was that of a senior Phon named Trondbarg. It was clear that Phon Trondbarg did know what was going on. He discussed Telzey's Pehanron project in polite detail but with an air of nervous detachment. It had been indicated to the Institute that she was a special agent of the Service, and that her research here was for form's sake only.

The interview didn't take long. Her credentials would be processed, and she was to return in four hours. She would have access then to normally restricted materials and be able to obtain other information as required. In effect, she was being given a nearly free run of the Institute, which was the purpose. Unless there were other developments, much of the Service's immediate attention would be focussed on the areas and personnel associated with the Tongi Phon's psi technology projects. The Phon leadership didn't like it but had no choice. They would have liked it less if they'd suspected that mind shields now would start coming quietly undone. The Service wanted to find out who around here was controlled and in what manner.

Some form of counteraction by the concealed opposition might be expected. Preparations were being made for it, and Telzey's personal warning system was one part of the preparations.

She returned to the Luerral Circuit and her hotel room alone except for her unnoticeable Service escorts, spent the next two hours asleep to get herself shifted over to the local time system, then dressed in a Tinokti fashion item, a sky-blue belted jacket of military cut and matching skirt, and had a belated breakfast in a stratosphere restaurant of the hotel. Back in the Great Lobby, she began to retrace the route to the Tongi Phon Institute she'd followed with Phon Hajugan some five hours ago. A series of drop shafts took her to a scenic link with swift-moving slideways; then there was a three-portal shift to the southern hemisphere where the Institute's major structures were located. She moved on through changing patterns of human traffic until she reached the ninth portal from the Great Lobby. On the far side of that portal, she stopped with a catch in her breath, spun about, found herself looking at a blank wall, and turned again.

Her mental contact with Gudast was gone. The portal had shifted her into a big, long, high-ceilinged room, empty and silent. She hadn't passed through any such room with Phon Hajugan. She should have exited here instead into the main passage of a shopping center.

She touched the wall through which she'd stepped an instant ago—as solid now as it looked. A one-way portal. The room held the peculiar air of blankness, a cave of stillness about the mind, which said it was psi-blocked and that the blocking fields were close by. Watching a large closed door at the other end of the room, Telzey clicked on the bracelet communicator. No response from the Service. . . . No response either, a moment later, from the Luerral ring key!

89

She'd heard that in the complexities of major portal systems, it could happen that a shift became temporarily distorted and one emerged somewhere else than one had intended to go. But that hadn't happened here. There'd been people directly ahead of her, others not many yards behind, her Service escorts among them, and no one else had portaled into this big room which was no part of the Luerral Circuit.

So it must be a trap—and a trap set up specifically for her along her route from the hotel room to the Tongi Phon Institute. As she reached the portal some observer had tripped the mechanisms which flicked in another exit for the instant needed to bring her to the room. If the Service still had a fix on the tracking device they'd given they would have recognized what had happened and be zeroing in on her now, but she had an unpleasantly strong conviction that whoever had cut her off so effectively from psi and communicator contacts also had considered the possibility of a tracking device and made sure it wouldn't act as one here.

The room remained quiet. A strip of window just below the ceiling ran along the wall on her left, showing patches of blue sky and tree greenery outside. It was far out of her reach, and if she found something that let her climb up to it, there was no reason to think it would be possible to get through that window. But she started cautiously forward. The room was L-shaped; on her right, the wall extended not much more than two thirds of its length before it cornered.

She could sense nothing but wasn't sure no one was waiting behind the corner for her until she got there. No one was. That part of the room was as bare as the other. At the end of it was a second closed door, a smaller one.

She turned back toward the first door, checked, skin crawling. Mind screens had contracted abruptly into a hard shield. One of *them* had come into this psi-blocked structure.

One or more of them. . . .

The larger door opened seconds later. Three tall people came into the room.

11

Telzey's continuing automatic reaction told her the three were psis of the type she'd conditioned herself to detect and recognize. Whatever they were, they had nothing resembling the bulk and massive structure of the Elaigar mind masters she'd studied in the old Nalakian records. They might be nearly as tall. The smallest, in the rich blue cloak and hood of a Sparan woman, must measure at least seven feet, and came barely up to the shoulders of her companions who wore the corresponding gray cloaks of Sparan men. Veils, golden for the woman, white for the men, concealed their faces below the eyes and fell to their chests.

But, of course, they weren't Sparans. Telzey had looked into Sparan minds. They probably were the Hub's most widespread giant strain, should have the average sprinkling of psi ability. They weren't an organization of psis. Their familiar standardized dressing practices simply provided these three with an effective form of concealment.

Telzey, heart racing, smiled at them.

"I hope I'm not trespassing!" she told them. "I was in the Luerral Hotel just a minute ago and have no idea how I got here! Can you tell me how to get back?"

The woman said in an impersonal voice, "I'm sure you're quite aware you're not here by accident. We'll take you presently to some people who want to see you. Now stand still while I search you."

She'd come up as she spoke, removing her golden gloves. Telzey stood still. The men had turned to the left along the wall, and a recess was suddenly in sight there . . . some portal arrangement. The recess seemed to be a large, half-filled storage closet. The men began bringing items out of it, while the woman searched Telzey quickly. The communicator and the Service's tracking device disappeared under the blue cloak. The woman took nothing else. She straightened again, said, "Stay where you are," and turned to join her companions who now were packing selected pieces of equipment into two carrier cases they'd taken from the closet. They worked methodically but with some haste, occasionally exchanging a few words in a language Telzey didn't know. Finally they snapped the cases shut, began to remove their Sparan veils and cloaks.

Telzey watched them warily. Her first sight of their faces was jarring. They were strong handsome faces with a breed similarity between them. But there was more than a suggestion there of the cruel cat masks of Nalakia. They'd needed the cover of the Sparan veil to avoid drawing attention to themselves.

The bodies were as distinctive. The woman, now in trunks, boots and short-sleeved shirt, as were the men, a gun belt fastened about her, looked slender with her height and length of limb, but layers of well-defined muscle shifted along her arms and legs as she moved. Her neck was a round strong column, the sloping shoulders correspondingly heavy, and there was a great depth of rib cage, drawing in sharply to the flat waist. She differed from the human standard as a strain of animals bred for speed or fighting might differ from other strains of the same species. Her companions were male counterparts, larger, more heavily muscled.

There'd been no trace of a mental or emotional impression from any of them; they were closely screened. The door at the end of the room opened now, and a third man of the same type came in. He was dressed almost as the others were, but everything he wore was dark green; and instead of a gun, a broad knife swung in its scabbard from his belt. He glanced at Telzey, said something in their language. The woman looked over at Telzey.

"Who are you?" Telzey asked her.

The woman said, "My name is Kolki Ming. I'm afraid there's no time for questions. We have work to do." She indicated the third man. "Tscharen will be in charge of you at present."

"We'll leave now," Tscharen told Telzey.

They were in a portal circuit. Once out of the room where Telzey had been trapped, they used no more doors. The portal sections through which they passed were small ones, dingy by contrast with the Luerral's luxuries, windowless interiors where people once had lived. Lighting and other automatic equipment still functioned; furnishings stood about. But there was a general air of long disuse. Psi blocks tangibly enclosed each section.

The portals weren't marked in any way, but Tscharen moved on without hesitation. They'd reach a wall and the wall would seem to dissolve about and before them; and they'd be through it, somewhere else—a somewhere else which didn't look very different from the section they'd just left. After the sixth portal shift, Tscharen turned into a room and unlocked and opened a wall cabinet.

A viewscreen had been installed in the cabinet. He manipulated the settings, and a brightly lit and richly furnished area, which might have been the reception room of some great house, appeared in the screen. There was no one in sight; the screen was silent. Tscharen studied the room for perhaps a minute, then switched off the screen, closed and locked the cabinet, motioned to Telzey and turned to leave. She followed.

They passed through two more portals. The second one took them into the big room of the viewscreen. They'd moved on a few steps across thick carpeting when Tscharen whirled abruptly. Telzey had a glimpse of a gun in his hand, saw him drop sideways. Someone landed with a harsh yell on the floor behind her, and a great hand gripped the back of her jacket below the collar. For a moment, a face stared down into hers. Then she was tossed aside with careless violence, and when she looked up from the carpeting, the giants were coming in through a doorspace at the far end of the room.

They moved like swift animals. She had barely time to scramble to her feet before they were there. One of them caught her arm, held her in a rock-hard grip, but the immediate attention of the group was on Tscharen. They crouched about him, shifting quickly back and forth. He'd recovered from whatever had knocked him out, was struggling violently. There were short angry shouts. Gusts of savage emotion boiled up, a battering of psi energies. Telzey's gaze flicked to the wall through which they'd stepped. Grips were fastened to it above the point where the portal had opened briefly. That was where Tscharen's attacker had clung, waiting. So these others had known he was coming along that route, or that someone was coming, and had laid an ambush.

The psi tumult ebbed out. They began to separate, get to their feet. She saw Tscharen lying face down, hands fastened behind his back, trussed up generally and motionless. Two remained beside him. The others turned toward Telzey, spreading out in a semicircle.

She swallowed carefully. More than a dozen stared at her, faces showing little expression at the moment. They were dressed in the same sort of dark green outfit as Tscharen, belted with guns and knives. The majority were of his type. Two of them, slighter, smaller-boned, were females.

But four in the group were not at all of the same type. They stood not many inches taller than the rest but were much more hugely designed throughout. They were, in fact, unmistakably what the old records had told about and shown—the psi ogres of Nalakia, the Elaigar.

One of these rumbled something to the lesser giant holding Telzey's arm. Thought patterns flickered for a moment through her awareness. She had the impression they didn't quite know what to make of the fact that she'd been in Tscharen's company.

She glanced toward the ogre who'd spoken. His brooding eyes narrowed. A mind probe stabbed at her.

Her shield blocked it.

Interest flared in the broad face. The others stirred, went quiet again.

So now they knew she was a psi.

Another probe came from the Elaigar, heavy and hard, testing the shield in earnest. It held. Some of the others began to grin. He grunted, in annoyance now, returned with a ramming thrust. Telzey slammed a bolt back at him, struck heavy shielding; and his eyes went wide with surprise. There was a roar of laughter. As psi mentalities, the great Elaigar seemed the same as

Tscharen's kind; she could make out no difference between them.

The noise ended abruptly. Faces turned toward the doorspace and the group shifted position, hands moving toward guns and knife hilts. Telzey followed their gaze. Hot fright jolted through her.

An animal stood in the room thirty feet away, small red eyes fixed on her. Thick-bodied, with massive head and forelimbs—one of their teleporting killers. It didn't move, but its appearance and stare were infinitely menacing. The giants themselves clearly weren't at ease in its presence.

It vanished.

Simultaneously, a voice spoke harshly from the doorway and another huge Elaigar strode into the room, followed by a humanoid creature in green uniform. It was a moment before Telzey realized the newcomer was female. There was little to distinguish her physically from the males of her type here. But something did distinguish her—something like a blaze of furious energy which enlivened the brutal features in their frame of shaggy black hair. Through her shield, Telzey felt a powerful mind sweep toward her, then abruptly withdraw. The giantess glanced at her as she approached, said something to the attendant humanoid, then turned toward Tscharen and addressed the others in a hard deep voice. The attitude of the group indicated she held authority among them.

The humanoid stopped before Telzey, took an instrument from one of his uniform pockets, thumbed open the cover, held the instrument to his mouth, pronounced a few high-pitched sentences, closed the device and replaced it. He looked up at the giant holding Telzey by the arm, and the giant growled a few words and moved off. The humanoid looked at Telzey. She looked at him.

Except for the fact that he wasn't much taller than she, his appearance was no more reassuring than that of the giants. The large round head and the hands were covered by skin like plum-colored velvet. The two eyes set wide apart in the head were white circles with black dots as pupils. There were no indications of ears, nostrils, or other sense organs. The mouth was a long straight lipless line. A variety of weapons and less readily definable devices were attached to the broad belt about the flat body.

The creature unclipped two of the belt gadgets now, stepped up to Telzey and began running them over her clothes. She realized she was being searched again and stood still. Plum-face was methodical and thorough. Everything he found he looked over briefly and stuffed into one of his pockets, winding up by pulling the Luerral ring key from Telzey's finger and adding it to the other items. Then he returned the search devices to his belt and spoke to somebody who was now standing behind Telzey. The somebody moved around into view.

Another kind of alien. This one was also about Telzey's size, wore clothing, walked upright on two legs. Any physical resemblance to humanity ended there. It had a head like that of a soft-shelled green bug, jaws hinged side to side. A curved band of yellow circles across the upper part of the face seemed to be eyes. What was visible of arms and legs, ending in the bony hands and narrow, shod feet, was reedy and knobjointed, the same shade of green as the head.

This creature didn't look at Telzey but simply stood there. Telzey guessed Plum-face had summoned it to the room with his communicator. Two of the group had picked up Tscharen now and were carrying him from the room. The giantess snapped out some command. The rest started toward the doorspace. She watched them leave, then turned abruptly. Telzey felt a thrill of alarm as the monster came up. The Elaigar spoke, a few short words.

The green alien at once told Telzey softly, in perfect translingue, "You are in the presence of Stiltik, who is a High Commander of the Elaigar. I'm to translate her instructions to you—and I advise you most urgently to do whatever she says, with no hesitation."

The jaws hadn't moved, but a short tube protruded from the front of the stalklike neck. The voice had come from there. The end of the tube was split, forming flexible lips with a fleshy blue tongue tip between them.

The harsh voice of Stiltik, High Commander of the Elaigar, broke in. The green alien resumed quickly. "You must open your mind to Stiltik. Do it immediately."

But that was the last thing she should do. Telzey said unsteadily, "Open my mind? I don't know what she means."

Bug-face translated. Stiltik, eyes fixed hard on Telzey, growled a brief response. The green creature, seeming almost in distress, said, "Stiltik says you're lying. Please don't defy her! She's very quick to anger."

Telzey shook her head helplessly.

"But it's impossible! I—"

She broke off. This time, Stiltik hadn't waited for translation. Psi pressure clamped about Telzey's shield, tightened like a great fist. She gave a startled gasp. There was no need to pretend being frightened; she was afraid enough of Stiltik. But not of this form of attack. Her shield had stood up under the crushing onslaught of a great psi machine. As far as she knew, no living mind could produce similar forces.

And in not too many seconds, Stiltik appeared to understand she would accomplish nothing in that manner.

The pressure ended abruptly. She stared down at Telzey, made a snorting sound, leaned forward. The mouth smiled in murderous anger; and the huge hands reached out with blurring speed, gripped Telzey, went knowingly to work.

Telzey was reminded in an instant then that when pain is excruciating enough there is no outcry, because lungs and throat seem paralyzed. She could have blocked out most of it, but Stiltik might be in a killing fury, and pain now offered a means of escape. It flowed through her like bursts of fire leaping up and combining. Her mind dimmed in shock, and she found herself lying on the floor, shaking, shield tight-locked. Stiltik roared out something high above her. Then there were footsteps, moving off. Then darkness, rolling in.

12

She decided presently that she hadn't been unconscious very long, though she hurt a great deal less
than she'd expected to be hurting when she woke up.
She kept her eyes shut; she wasn't alone. She was lying
on her side, with something like a hard cot underneath.
The area was psi-blocked, and evidently it was a large
structure because she had no feeling of blocking fields
close by. Her warning mechanisms indicated one or
more minds of the Elaigar type around.

Something touched her lightly in an area which was
still sufficiently painful. Around the touch pain began to
diminish, as if a slow wave of coolness were spreading
out and absorbing it. So she was being treated for the
mauling she'd had from Stiltik—very effectively treated,
to judge by the way she felt.

Now to determine who was in the vicinity.

Telzey canceled the alerting mechanisms, lightened
her shielding, reached out cautiously. After a minute or
two, vague thought configurations touched her awareness. Nonpsi and alien they were—she could develop
that contact readily.

Next, sense of a psi shield. Whoever used it wasn't far
away. . . .

The device which had been draining pain from her withdrew, leaving a barely noticeable residual discomfort where it had been. It touched another sore spot, resumed its ministrations. A mingling of the alien thoughts accompanied the transfer. They were beginning to seem comprehensible—a language half understood. The xenotelepathic quality of her mind was at work.

Her screens abruptly drew tight. There'd been a momentary wash of Elaigar thought. Gone now. But—

Fury swirled about her, surging from a telepathic mind which seemed completely unshielded, nakedly open. An Elaigar mind. The rage, whatever caused it, had nothing to do with Telzey. The giant didn't appear aware that she was in the area.

The impression faded again, didn't return. Telzey waited a minute, slid a light probe toward the psi shield she'd touched. She picked up no indication of anything there. It was a good tight shield, and that was all. Psi shield installed over a nonpsi mind? It should be that.

She left a watch thought there, a trace of awareness. If the shield opened or softened, she'd know, be back for a further look. She returned to the alien nonpsi thought patterns. By now, it was obvious that they were being produced by two minds of the same species.

It was a gentle, unsuspicious species. Telzey moved easily into both minds. One was Stiltik's green-bug interpreter, named Couse; a female. Couse's race called themselves the Tanvens. Her companion was Sasar, male; a physician. Kind Bug-faces! They had problems enough of their own, no happy future ahead. But at the moment, they were feeling sorry for the human who had been mishandled by Stiltik and were doing what they could to help her.

They might help more than they realized. Telzey put taps on their memory banks which would feed general information to hers without further attention, began dropping specific questions into the nonresisting awarenesses.

Responses came automatically.

After she lost consciousness, she'd been brought here by Essu. Essu was Plum-face, the uniformed humanoid. He was a Tolant, chief of Stiltik's company of Tolants. Stiltik had ordered Couse to summon Sasar, the most skilled physician in her command, to tend to the human's injuries and revive her. She was a valuable captive who was to remain in Essu's charge then, until Stiltik sent for her. The Tanvens didn't know when that would be. But it might be a considerable while, because Stiltik was interrogating the other captive now.

Essu was waiting in the passage outside this room. So he was the wearer of the psi shield, though the Tanvens knew nothing of that. Stiltik presumably had equipped him with one to safeguard her secrets from other psi minds. Essu acted as her general assistant, frequently as her executioner and torturer. A cruel, cunning creature! The Tanvens feared him almost as much as they feared Stiltik.

They didn't know there was an Elaigar in the vicinity. As far as they were aware, they were alone in this circuit section with Essu and Telzey. It had been a hospital facility once, but was now rarely used. The bad-tempered giant might be a good distance away from them.

Telzey shifted her line of questioning. The Elaigar had enslaved members of many races besides Tanvens and Tolants. Giants of Stiltik's kind were called Sattarams and supplied almost all the leaders. The lesser Elaigar were Otessans. Tscharen belonged to a third variety called Alattas, who looked like Otessans and now and then were caught masquerading as them, as Tscharen had been. The Alattas were enemies of the Sattarams and Otessans, and Couse and Sasar had heard rumors that an Alatta force was at present trying to invade the circuit.

At that point, Telzey drew back from the Tanven minds, leaving only the memory taps in place. For immediate practical purposes, Couse and Sasar had a limited usefulness. They were unable to think about the Elaigar in any real detail. When she tried to pin them down, their thought simply blurred. They knew only as much about their masters as they needed to know to perform their duties.

Similarly, they had a frustratingly vague picture of the portal circuit the Elaigar had occupied on Tinokti. It appeared to be an extensive system. They were familiar with a limited part of it and had been supplied with key packs which permitted them to move about within that area. They had no curiosity about what lay beyond. In particular, they'd never wondered about the location of exits from the circuit to the world outside. Escape was something they didn't think about; it was a meaningless concept. The Elaigar had done a thorough job of conditioning them.

She could control the Tanvens easily, but it wouldn't gain her anything.

Plum-face was the logical one to get under control. He was in charge of her, and the fact that he was Stiltik's assistant could make him the most useful sort of confederate. However, the psi shield presented a problem. Telzey thought she could work through it, given time enough. But Stiltik might show up and discover what she was doing. Stiltik would make very sure then that she didn't get a chance to try other tricks.

She decided to wait a little with Essu. The shield might be less inflexible than it seemed at present. Meanwhile, there was a fourth mind around. The Elaigar mind.

She considered, not liking that notion too well. There'd been occasional impressions which indicated this particular Elaigar remained careless about his shielding. He didn't seem to be aware of any of them here. But if he suspected he was being probed, he'd start hunting around the limited psi-blocked area for the prober.

She thought finally she should take the chance—he was preoccupied and angry.

She reached out gradually toward the Elaigar awareness. Her concern lessened then. There was a screen there but so loosely held it might as well have been nonexistent. The thought currents behind it shifted in fluctuating disorder over a quivering undercurrent of anger. Insane, she realized. A sick old male sunk deep in derangement, staring at problems for which there was no real solution, rousing himself periodically to futile fury.

Telzey eased in a memory tap, paused—

Stiltik! She slipped out of the Elaigar mind, flicked her watch thought away from Essu's shield. Tight went her own shield then.

Stiltik was present, after a fashion. Somewhere in this psi-blocked structure, a portal had opened and she'd stepped through. A signal now touched Essu's shield, and the shield went soft. Not many seconds later, it hardened again. Some instruction had been given the Tolant.

But Stiltik wasn't yet gone. Telzey sensed a search thought about. She could hide from it by ceasing all psi activity, but that simply would tell Stiltik she was conscious. She allowed a normal trickle of psi energy to drift out, let Stiltik's mind find her behind her shield.

Something touched the shield, tested it with a slow pressure probe, which got nowhere, withdrew. A hard, dizzying bolt slammed suddenly at her then; another. That sort of thing shouldn't help an unconscious patient make a faster recovery, Telzey thought. Perhaps Stiltik had the same reflection; she let it go at that. When Telzey made a cautious scan of the area a minute or two later, there was no trace of the giantess in the structure.

Essu appeared in the entrance to the room and wanted to know how much longer it was going to take Sasar to get the human awake and in good enough shape so she could walk. Telzey followed the talk through Couse's mind. Couse was acting as interpreter again. Essu didn't understand the Tanven tongue, nor Sasar that of the Tolants or Elaigar. The physician was alarmed by Essu's indications of impatience, but replied bravely enough. Couse had given him Stiltik's instructions: he was to make sure the patient retained no dangerous injuries before he released her to Essu, and he couldn't be sure of it yet. She appeared to be healing well and rapidly, but her continuing unconsciousness was not a good sign. Essu pronounced a few imprecations in his high sharp voice, resumed his post in the passage.

The signal which caused Essu's shield to relax presently reached it again. Essu wasn't aware of it, but the shield softened in mechanical obedience. This time, it was Telzey's probe which slipped through. She'd reproduced the signal as carefully as she could, but hadn't been too sure it was an exact copy. Evidently she'd come close enough—and now for some quick and nervous work! If Stiltik happened to return before she got organized here, it wasn't likely she could escape discovery.

That part of it then turned out to be easier than she'd expected. Essu's mind already was well organized for her purpose. She flicked through installed telepathic channels to indicated control points. By the time she'd scanned the system, knew she understood it, most of the Tolant's concepts were becoming comprehensible to her. She checked on the immediately important point. What was he to do with her after she came awake and Sasar pronounced her condition to be satisfactory?

Response came promptly. Essu would take her to Stiltik's private lockup, inform Stiltik of the fact, and stay with Telzey until Stiltik wanted her. The lockup was a small sealed circuit section known only to Stiltik and Essu. Stiltik believed the human psi would be an important catch. She didn't want her enemies to hear about it until she'd finished squeezing the truth from the Alatta, and had searched through Telzey's mind for information she could turn to political advantage. It appeared Stiltik was engaged in a power struggle with Boragost, the other High Commander in the Elaigar circuit.

Essu's shield hardened again until it appeared solidly locked, though a really close investigation would have revealed that contact remained now between his mind and Telzey's. Telzey didn't want to break that contact unless she had to. The Tolant should turn out to be as useful as she'd thought, and she had to do a good deal of work on him before he'd be ready for use—which made it time to be restored officially to consciousness and health. Once Stiltik was informed the prisoner was safely in the lockup, she should be satisfied to leave it to Essu to see Telzey stayed there.

And that would be essential for a while.

A thought whispered, "I know you're planning to escape from the Elaigar! Would you permit me to accompany you?"

For an instant Telzey froze in shock. That had been a human thought. Otherwise there hadn't been—and still wasn't—the slightest indication of another human being around. She flicked back a question. "Where are you?"

"Not far away. I could be with you in a minute."

Now she'd noticed something. "You're human?" she asked.

"Of course. My name is Thrakell Dees."

"It seems to me," Telzey remarked, "there's something here that could be part of the two Tanven minds I've been in contact with—or perhaps a third Tanven mind. But if you look closely, it's only the impression of a Tanven mind."

Silence for a moment. "A projected form of concealment," Thrakell Dees's thought said then. "One of the means I've developed to stay alive in this cave of devils."

"How do you happen to be in the circuit?"

"I was trapped here over six years ago when the Elaigar suddenly appeared. I've never found a way to get out."

Telzey gave Essu's mind a questioning prod. "You mean you don't know where the exits to Tinokti are?" she asked Thrakell Dees.

"I have an approximate idea of where they should be. However, they're very securely guarded."

Yes, wild humans, Essu was thinking. Quite a number of humans had managed to hide out in the circuit in the early period. Hunting them had been good sport for a while. There were occasional indications that a few still survived, skulking about in unused sections.

"What happened to the other human beings in the circuit?" Telzey asked Thrakell Dees.

"The Elaigar and their serfs killed most of them at once. I myself was nearly caught often enough in those days. Only my psi abilities saved me. Later I learned other methods of avoiding the creatures. The circuit is very large, and only a part of it is occupied by them."

"Is anyone left besides you?"

"No, I'm the last. A year ago I encountered another survivor, but he was killed soon afterwards. The Elaigar have brought in captured humans from time to time, but none ever escaped and few lived long. Today I learned from a serf mind that Stiltik had trapped a human psi. I began looking for you, thinking I might be of help. But it seems you have your own plans. I suggest we cooperate. I can be very useful."

"What do you know about my plans?" Telzey asked.

"Nothing directly. Your thoughts were too closely screened. But I've been following the responses you drew from the Tanvens. They indicate you intend to attempt an escape."

"All right," Telzey said. "I will try to escape. If you want to come along, fine. We should be able to help each other. But keep out of the way now, because I'll be busy. The Tolant will be taking me somewhere else soon. Can you follow without letting him see you?"

"I'm rarely seen unless I want to be." His reply seemed to hold a momentary odd note of amusement. "I can follow you easily in the general circuit. I have keys for some sealed areas, too. Not, of course, for all of them."

"We'll be in a sealed area for a while, but we'll come back out," Telzey told him. "Let's not talk any more now. I'm going to wake up."

She dissolved the memory taps in the Tanven minds and that of the old Elaigar, stirred about on the cot, then opened her eyes, looked up into Couse's green face and glanced over at Sasar who had drawn back a trifle when she began to move.

"What's happened?" Telzey asked. She looked at Couse again, blinked. "You're the interpreter. . . ."

"Yes, I am," said Couse.

Sasar said in the Tanven tongue, "What is the human saying? Ask her how she feels," the thoughts carrying through the meaningless sound. Essu, hearing the voices, had appeared in the entrance again and was watching the group.

Couse relayed the question, adding that Sasar had been acting as Telzey's physician after she had been injured. Telzey shifted her shoulders, twisted her neck, touched herself cautiously.

"He's a very good physician!" she told Couse. "I'm still aching a little here and there, but that's all."

Couse translated that twice, first for Sasar, and then for Essu, who had some understanding of translingue but not enough to be certain of what Telzey was saying.

"The human aches a little!" Essu repeated. "It's awake and it can walk, so it's healthy enough. Tell your healer he's relieved of his responsibility, and be on your way, both of you!"

The Tanvens left quickly and quietly. There was a belt of woven metal fastened around Telzey's waist, with a strap of the same material attached to the belt. The other end of the strap was locked to the wall beyond the cot. Essu unfastened it now and brought Telzey flopping off the cot to the floor with a sudden haul on the strap. A short green rod appeared in Essu's free hand then. He pointed it at Telzey's legs, and she felt two sharp insect stings.

"Get *hup!*" said Essu, practicing his translingue.

She got up. He shoved her hands through loops in the

back of the belt, and tightened the loops on her wrists. Then he took the end of the strap and left the room with the prisoner in tow. The Tanvens had turned right along the passage. Essu turned left. A closed door blocked the end, and as they approached it, he took something from his pocket, touched the device to the doorlock. The door swung open. They went through into an extension of the passage, and the door swung shut on its lock behind them.

There was a sudden heavy stirring in Telzey's mind . . . Elaigar thoughts. The old male was coming alert. She realized suddenly he could hear them. This seemed to be his area—and Essu was unaware it had an occupant. There was a heavily curtained doorspace in the wall just ahead—

As they came up to it, the curtains were swept aside and a huge Sattaram loomed above them. She felt Essu's shock of alarm. Then the Elaigar's hand flicked out with the same startling speed Stiltik had shown. Telzey was struck across the side of the head, went stumbling back against the wall. With her hands fastened behind her, she couldn't get her balance back quickly enough and sat down.

It hadn't been too hard a blow—from the giant's point of view no more than a peevish cuff. But he wasn't finished. He'd whipped a heavy knife from his belt, and was looking down at her. A human! He'd had no sport for too long a time. His lip curled, drawing up from big yellowed teeth.

Telzey felt dismay rather than fright. Fast-moving they were—but this Elaigar's mind was open to her and he wasn't aware of the fact. She could slash psi-death into it through the sloppily held screens before the knife touched her skin.

But that could cost her too much—Essu, for one

111

thing. He knew she was a psi, and if a Sattaram died in the act of attacking her, he wasn't likely to consider it a coincidence. He'd try to get the information to Stiltik at once. She was beginning to develop some degree of control over Essu but was unsure of its effect on the unfamiliar Tolant mind. In any case, she couldn't control him enough at present to override any sudden strong motivation. She might have to kill him in the same manner.

It was Essu who saved matters then.

He'd hung on to the end of the strap when Telzey fell, but he stood as far from her and the Elaigar as he possibly could, arm stretched out, eyes averted from both, as if detaching himself completely from this unpleasant situation. When he spoke in the Elaigar language, he appeared to be addressing the wall before him.

"Glorious One—is it your intention to deprive *Stiltik* of prey?"

Slow surge of alarm in the old Sattaram. Stiltik? The hate-filled eyes grew vague. He swung his ponderous head toward the Tolant, stared a long moment, then turned and lumbered back through the doorspace. The curtains swung shut behind him.

Essu was beside Telzey, jerking her up to her feet.

"Come! Come!" he hissed in translingue.

They hurried quietly on along the passage.

13

Essu, though a bold being, had been shaken by the encounter, and it continued to preoccupy him. As a rule, the green uniform of Stiltik's servants was safeguard enough against mistreatment by other Elaigar even when they weren't aware that he was her valued assistant. But when age came on them, they grew morose and became more savage and unpredictable than ever. The great knife might have turned swiftly on him after it finished Telzey; and to use one of the weapons on his belt then would have been almost as dangerous for Essu as not using them. Self-defense was no excuse for killing or injuring one of the masters.

Much greater, however, had been his fear of facing Stiltik after letting her prisoner get killed. He blamed Telzey for putting him in such a terrible predicament, and was simmering with vengeful notions. But he didn't let that distract him from choosing the rest of their route with great care.

Telzey, aware of Essu's angry spite, was too busy to give it much consideration. Being involved in Stiltik's business, the Tolant knew a great deal more about the circuit and what went on in it than the Tanvens; she was getting additional information now. The four Alattas involved in bringing her into the circuit had been operating here as Otessans—Tscharen and the woman Kolki Ming in Stiltik's command, the other two in Boragost's. Tscharen was permanently stationed in the circuit; the others were frequently given outside assignments. Stiltik had been watching Tscharen for some time; her spy system indicated he was occasionally engaged in off-duty activities in unused sealed areas, and she had her scientists set up traps. His secret meeting with the other three and the human they'd brought into the circuit with them was observed on a scanner. Knowing now that she dealt with Alatta infiltrators, Stiltik sprang her traps. But so far only Tscharen and the human had been caught. The others had withdrawn into sealed sections, and a search force of Elaigar and Tolants sent to dig them out had run into difficulties and returned empty-handed.

This obviously was a vast portal system which might almost rival the Luerral in its ramifications. Essu had seen a good deal of it on Stiltik's business, but by no means every part; and he was no more aware of exits to the planet or able to consider the possibility of making use of them than the Tanvens. How the Elaigar could have taken over such a complex, and killed off the humans living there, without creating a stir on Tinokti, was something else he didn't know. The answer might be found in the material Telzey's memory tap had drawn from the old Elaigar, but she couldn't spare time to start sorting through that at present.

None of the sections along their route seemed to be in use by the Elaigar. It was like moving about parts of a deserted city through which a marauding army had swept, stripping all removable equipment from some points while others remained overlooked. Where maintenance machinery still functioned completely, it often appeared that the former occupants might have left only the day before.

But all was silent; all was psi-blocked. Even where daylight or starshine filled empty courtyards or flowering gardens, impenetrable energy screens lay between them and the unaware world outside.

The arrangements of Stiltik's lockup were much like those in the series of sections through which Tscharen had taken Telzey. It lay well within a sealed area, and its connecting portals showed no betraying gleam, remained barely visible for the moment it took Essu and Telzey to pass them. The Tolant shoved her eventually into a small room, slammed and locked the door. She stayed with him mentally as he went off down a passage to report by communicator to Stiltik, who might be on the far side of Tinokti now.

He returned presently. The Elaigar commander had indicated it still could be several hours before she sent for them. When he opened the door, the prisoner was leaning against the wall. Essu went over to the single large cot the room contained, sat down on it, and fixed his round white eyes on the human.

Telzey looked at him. Torture and killing were the high points of Essu's existence. She didn't particularly blame him. Tolants regarded warfare as the natural way of life, and when a group found itself temporarily out of neighbors, it relieved the monotony by internal blood feuds. Under such circumstances, the exercise of cruelty, the antidote to fear, became a practical virtue. Elaigar service had done nothing to diminish the tendency in Essu.

If he hadn't been required to take on responsibility for the human captive, he would have been assisting Stiltik now in her interrogation of Tscharen. That pleasure was denied him. The human, in addition, very nearly had placed him in the position of becoming a candidate for Stiltik's lingering attentions himself. Clearly, she owed him something! He couldn't do much to her, but Stiltik wouldn't begrudge him some minor amusements to help while away the waiting period.

Very deliberately then, Essu brought out the green device with which he'd jabbed Telzey before, and let her look at it.

Telzey sighed. She was now supposed to display fear. Then, after she'd cringed sufficiently at the threat of the prod, the hot stings would begin. If necessary, she could shut out most of the pain and put up with that kind of treatment for quite a while. Essu wouldn't risk carrying it far enough to incapacitate her. But it seemed a good time to find out whether it was still necessary to put up with anything at all from him.

She sent a series of impulses through one of the control centers she'd secured in Essu's mind. Essu carefully turned the green rod down, pointed it at his foot. One of his fingers pressed a button. He jerked his foot aside and uttered a shrill yelp. Then he quietly returned the rod to his pocket.

It was a good indication of solid control. However, she didn't feel quite sure of the Tolant. An unshielded telepathic mind which wasn't resisting might be taken over almost in moments by another psi, particularly if the other psi was of the same species. All required channels were wide open. A nontelepathic mind, even that of another human, could require considerable work. In Essu's mind, nontelepathic and nonhuman, there were many patterns which closely paralleled human ones. Others were quite dissimilar. Stiltik had left a kind of blueprint in there for Telzey to follow, but she didn't know whether she'd interpreted all the details of the blueprint correctly.

She put in some ten minutes of testing before she was certain. Essu performed perfectly. There was no reason to think he wouldn't continue to perform perfectly when he was no longer under direct control.

They left the sealed area together, moved on quickly. Stiltik wasn't likely to come looking for them soon, but as a start, Telzey wanted to put considerable distance between herself and the lockup. Some while later, she was on a narrow gallery overlooking a huge hall, watching Essu cross the hall almost two hundred yards below. He knew where he could pick up a set of circuit maps without drawing attention to himself, was on his way to get them. Dependable maps of the portal system was one of the things she was going to need. She'd kept one of Essu's weapons, a small gun which didn't demand too much experience with guns to be used effectively at close range. She also was keeping his key pack, except for the keys he needed for his present mission.

She followed him mentally. Essu knew what he was doing and it wouldn't occur to him to wonder why he was doing it. He'd simply serve her with mechanical loyalty, incapable of acting in any other way. As he reached the portal toward which he'd been headed and passed through it, his thought patterns vanished. But here, within the psi blocks enclosing the great hall and part of the structure behind Telzey, something else remained. The vague impression of a Tolant mentality.

So that veteran wild human Thrakell Dees had managed to follow them, as he'd said he would, and was now trying to remain unobtrusive! Telzey considered. Shortly after the encounter with the old Elaigar, she'd become aware of Thrakell's light, stealthy probe at her screens. She'd jabbed back irritatedly with psi and drawn a startled reaction. After that, Thrakell refrained from manifesting himself. She hadn't been sure until now that he was around.

He might, she thought, turn out to be more of a problem than a help. In any case, they'd have to have a definite understanding if they were to work together to reach a portal exit. He'd soon realize that Essu had left the area. Telzey decided to wait and see what he would do.

She settled herself on the gallery floor behind the balustrade, from where she could keep watch on the portal where Essu presently would reappear, and began bringing up information she'd tapped from the old Elaigar's mind and hadn't filtered through her awareness yet. She could spend some time on that now. Part of her attention remained on Thrakell's dimly shifting Tolant cover impressions.

The hodgepodge of information started to acquire some order as she let herself become conscious of it. The Elaigar's name was Korm. He'd been Suan Uwin once, a High Commander, who'd fallen into disgrace. . . .

She made some unexpected discoveries next.

They seemed a stranger variation of the human race than she'd thought, these Elaigar! Their individual life span was short—perhaps too short to have let them develop the intricate skills of civilization if they'd wanted to. As they considered it, however, mental and physical toil were equally unworthy of an Elaigar. They prided themselves on being the masters of those who'd acquired advanced civilized skills and were putting that knowledge now to Elaigar use.

She couldn't make out clearly what Korm's measurement of time came to in Federation units, but by normal human standards, he wasn't more than middle-aged, if that. As an Elaigar, he was very old. That limitation was a race secret, kept concealed from serfs. Essu and the Tanvens assumed Sattarams and Otessans were two distinct Elaigar strains. But one was simply the mature adult, the other the juvenile form, which ap-

118

parently made a rather abrupt transition presently to adulthood.

The Alattas? A debased subrace. It had lost the ability to develop into Sattarams, and it worked like serfs because it had no serfs. Beyond that, the Alattas were enemies who might threaten the entire Elaigar campaign in the human Federation—

Telzey broke off her review of Korm's muddled angry mind content.

Had there been some change in those fake Tolant impressions put out by Thrakell Dees? . . . Yes, there had! She came fully alert.

"Thrakell?"

No response. The impressions shifted slowly.

"You might as well start talking," she told him. "I know you're there!"

After a moment, his reply came sulkily. "You weren't very friendly a while ago!"

He didn't seem far away. Telzey glanced along the gallery, then over at the door through which she'd come out on it. Behind the door, a passage ran parallel to the gallery. Thrakell Dees probably was there.

She said, "I didn't think it was friendly of you either to try to get to my mind when you thought I might be too busy to notice! If we're going to work together, there can't be any more tricks like that."

A lengthy pause. The screening alien patterns blurred, reformed, blurred again.

"Where did you send the Tolant?" Thrakell Dees asked suddenly.

"He's getting something for me."

"What kind of thing?"

This time it was Telzey who didn't reply. Stalling, she thought. Her skin began to prickle. What was he up to?

She glanced uneasily up and down the gallery. He wasn't there. But—

Her breath caught softly.

It was as if she'd blinked away a blur on her vision.

She took Essu's gun from her jacket pocket, turned, pointed the gun toward the gallery wall on her right.

And there Thrakell Dees, moving very quietly toward her, barely twenty feet away, came to an abrupt halt, eyes widening in consternation.

"Yes, I see you now!" Telzey said between her teeth, cheeks hot with anger. "I know that not-there trick! And it won't work on me when I suspect it's being used."

Thrakell moistened his lips. He was a bony man of less than average height, who might be forty years of age. He wore shirt and trousers of mottle brown shades, a round white belt encircling his waist in two tight loops. He had small intent blue eyes, set deep under thick brows, and a high bulging forehead. His long hair was pulled sharply to the back of his head and tied there. A ragged beard framed the lower face.

"No need to point the gun at me," he said. He smiled, showing bad teeth. "I'm afraid I was trying to impress you with my abilities. I admit it was a thoughtless thing to do."

Telzey didn't lower the gun. She felt quite certain there'd been nothing thoughtless about that stealthy approach. He'd had a purpose; and whatever it had been, it wasn't simply to impress her with his abilities.

"Thrakell," she said, "just keep your hands in sight and sit down over there by the balustrade. You can help me watch the hall while I watch you. There're some things I want you to tell me about—but better not do anything at all to make me nervous before Essu gets back!"

He shrugged and complied. When he was settled on the floor to Telzey's satisfaction, she laid the gun down before her. Thrakell might be useful, but he was going to take watching, at least until she knew more about him.

He seemed anxious to make amends, answering her questions promptly and refraining from asking questions himself after she'd told him once there was no time for that now.

The picture she got of the Elaigar circuit was rather startling. What the Service was confronted with on Tinokti was a huge and virtually invisible fortress. The circuit had no official existence; there never had been a record of it in Tongi Phon files. Its individual sections were scattered about the planet, most of them buried among thousands of sections of other circuits, outwardly indistinguishable from them. If a section did happen to be identified and its force screens were overpowered, which could be no simple matter in populated areas, it would be cut automatically out of the circuit from a central control section, leaving searchers no farther than before. The control section itself lay deep underground. They'd have to start digging up Tinokti to locate it.

Then there was a device called the Vingarran, connected with the control section. Telzey had found impressions of it in the material drawn from Korm's mind. Korm knew how the Vingarran was used and hadn't been interested in knowing more. Thrakell couldn't add much. It was a development of alien technology, constructed by the Elaigar's serf scientists. It was like a superportal with a minimum range which made it unusable within the limited extent of a planet. Its original purpose might have been to provide interplanetary transportation. The Elaigar used it to connect the Tinokti circuit with spaceships at the fringes of the system. They came and went customarily by that method, though there were a number of portal exits to the planetary surface. They were in no way trapped here by the Service's investment of Tinokti.

"How could a circuit like that get set up in the first place?" Telzey asked.

Thrakell bared his teeth in an unpleasant grimace.

"Phons of the Institute planned it and had it done. Who else could have arranged it secretly?"

"Why did they do it?"

He shrugged. "It was their private kingdom. Whoever was brought into it, as I was one day, became their slave. Escape was impossible. Our Phon lords were responsible to no one and did as they pleased—until the Elaigar came. Then they were no more than their slaves and died with them."

Telzey reflected. "You've been able to tap Elaigar minds without getting caught at it?" she asked.

"I've done it on occasion," Thrakell said, "but I haven't tried it for some time. I made a nearly disastrous slip with a relatively inexperienced Otessan, and decided to discontinue the practice. An Elaigar mind is always dangerous—the creatures are suspicious of one another and alert for attempted probes and controls. Instead I maintain an information network of unshielded serfs. I can pick up almost anything I want to know from one or the other of them, without running risks." He added, "Of course, old Korm can be probed rather safely, as I imagine you discovered."

"Yes, I did," Telzey said. "Then you've never tried to control one of them?"

Thrakell looked startled. "That would be most inadvisable!"

"It might be." Telzey said, "By our standards, Korm isn't really old, is he?"

"Not at all!" Thrakell Dees seemed amused.

"Twenty-four Federation years, at most."

"They don't live any longer than *that?*" Telzey said.

"Few live even that long! One recurring satisfaction I've had here is to watch my enemies go lumbering down to death, one after the other, these past six years. Stiltik, at seventeen, is in her prime. Boragost, now twenty, is past his. And Korm exists only as an object lesson."

Telzey had seen that part vividly in Korm's jumbled recalls. Sattarams, male or female, weren't expected to outlive their vigor. When they began to weaken noticeably, they challenged younger and stronger Sattarams and died fighting. Those who appeared hesitant about it were taken to see Korm. He'd held back too long on issuing his final challenge, and had been shut away, left to deteriorate, his condition a warning to others who risked falling into the same error.

She learned that the Elaigar changed from the Otessan form to the adult one in their fourteenth year. That sudden drastic metamorphosis was also a racial secret. Otessans approaching the point left the circuit; those who returned as Sattarams weren't recognized by the serfs. Thrakell could add nothing to the information about the Alattas Telzey already had gathered. He knew Alatta spies had been captured in the circuit before this; they'd died by torture or in ritual combat with Sattaram leaders. There was a deadly enmity between the two obviously related strains.

On the subject of the location of the Elaigar home territories, he could offer only that they must be several months' travel from the Hub clusters. And Korm evidently knew no more. Space navigation was serf work, its details below an Elaigar's notice.

"Have they caught the three Alattas who got away from Stiltik yet?" Telzey asked.

There Thrakell was informed. He'd been listening around among his mental contacts before following Telzey to the hospital area. The three still had been at large at that time, and there seemed to be no immediate prospect of catching up with them. They'd proved to be expert portal technicians who'd sealed off sizable circuit areas by distorting portal patterns and substituting their own. Stiltik's portal specialists hadn't been able to handle the problem. The armed party sent after the three was equipped with copies of a key pack taken from Tscharen but had no better luck. The matter wasn't being discussed, and Thrakell Dees suspected not all of the hunters had returned.

"Stiltik would very much like to be able to announce that she's rounded up the infiltrators," he said. "It would add to her prestige which is high at present."

"Apparently Stiltik and Boragost—the Suan Uwin—don't get along very well?" Telzey said.

He laughed. "One of them will kill the other! Stiltik doesn't intend to wait much longer to become senior Suan Uwin, and she's generally rated now as the deadliest fighter in the circuit. The Elaigar make few of our nice distinctions between the sexes."

Boragost's qualities as a leader, it appeared, were in question. Stiltik had been pushing for a unified drive to clear the Alattas out of the Federation. She'd gained a large following. Boragost blocked the move, on the grounds that a major operation of the kind couldn't be carried out without alerting the Federation's humans to the presence of aliens. And now Boragost had committed a blunder which might have accomplished just that. "You know what dagens are?" Thrakell asked.

"Yes. The mind hounds. I saw Stiltik's when they caught me."

He shifted uncomfortably. "Horrible creatures! Fortunately, there're only three in the circuit at present because few Elaigar are capable of controlling them. A short while ago, Boragost fumbled a dagen kill outside the circuit."

Telzey nodded. "Four Phons in the Institute. That wasn't planned then?"

"Far from it! Only one of the Phons was to die, and that neither in the Institute nor in the presence of witnesses. But Boragost failed to verify the victim's exact whereabouts at the moment he released the mind hound, and the mind hound, of course, went where the Phon was. When it found him among others, it killed them, too. Stiltik's followers claim that was what brought the Psychology Service to Tinokti."

"It was," Telzey said. "How will they settle it?"

"Almost certainly through Stiltik's challenge to Boragost. The other high-ranking Sattarams in the Hub have been coming in with their staffs through the Vingarran Gate throughout the week. They'll decide whether Boragost's conduct under their codes entitles Stiltik to challenge. If it does, he must accept. If it doesn't, she'll be deprived of rank and returned to their home territories. The codes these creatures bind themselves by are iron rules. It's the only way they have to avoid major butcheries among the factions."

Telzey was silent a moment, blinking reflectively at him.

"Thrakell," she said, "when we met, you told me you were the last human left alive in the circuit."

His eyes went wary. "That's right."

"There's been someone besides us with a human mind in this section for some little while now," Telzey told him. "The name is Neto. Neto Nayne-Mel."

14

Thrakell Dees said quickly, "Have nothing to do with that creature! She's dangerously unbalanced! I didn't tell you about her because I was afraid you might think of letting her join us."

"I am letting her join us," Telzey said.

Thrakell shook his head violently. "I advise you strongly against it! Neto Nayne-Mel is unpredictable. I know that she's ambushed and killed two Elaigar. She could endanger us all with her hatreds!"

Telzey said, "I understand she was a servant of the Elaigar in the circuit for a couple of years before she managed to get away from them. I suppose that might leave someone a little unbalanced. She's got something for me. I told her to bring it here to the gallery."

Thrakell grimaced nervously. "Neto's threatened to shoot me if she finds me within two hundred yards of her!"

"Well, Thrakell," Telzey said, "she may have caught you trying to sneak up on her, like I did. But that won't count now. We're going to need one another's help to get out. Neto understands that."

Thrakell argued no further. He still looked badly upset, due in part perhaps to the fact that there'd been a mental exchange between Neto and Telzey of which he'd remained unaware.

A human being who was to stay alive and at large for any length of time in the Elaigar circuit would need either an unreasonable amount of luck or rather special qualities. Thrakell, along with the ability to project a negation of his physical presence, had mental camouflage, and xenotelepathy which enabled him to draw information from unsuspecting alien mentalities around him.

Neto was otherwise equipped. Her mind didn't shield itself, but its patterns could be perceived only by a degree of psi sensitivity which Thrakell Dees lacked, and the Elaigar evidently also lacked. She'd devised a form of physical concealment almost as effective as Thrakell's. Her other resources were quick physical re-actions and a natural accuracy with a gun which she'd discovered after escaping from her masters. She'd killed four Elaigar since then, not two. Her experiences had, in fact, left her somewhat unbalanced, but not in a way Telzey felt at all concerned about.

A few minutes later, Neto stepped out suddenly on the gallery a hundred feet away and started toward them. The figure they saw was that of a Fossily mechanic, one of the serf people in the circuit—a body of slim human type enclosed by a fitted yellow coverall which left only the face exposed. The face was a mask of vivid black and yellow lines. Neto was almost within speaking distance before the human features concealed by the Fossily face pattern began to be discernible.

That was the disguise Neto had adopted for herself. Fossily mechanics, with their tool kits hung knapsackwise behind their shoulders, were employed almost everywhere in the circuit and drew no attention in chance encounters. Moreover, they had a species odor profoundly offensive to Elaigar nostrils. Their overall suits were chemically impregnated to hide it; and the resulting sour but tolerable smell also covered the human scent. A second yellow tool bag swung by its straps from Neto's gloved left hand. In it was a Fossily suit for Telzey, and black and yellow face paint.

Essu returned not long afterwards. Telzey touched his mind as he appeared in the portal down in the great hall, and knew he'd carried out his assignment. A pack of circuit diagram maps was concealed under his uniform jacket. He hadn't let himself be seen.

He joined them on the gallery, blandly accepting the presence of two wild humans and the fact that Telzey and Neto were disguised as Fossily mechanics. Telzey looked at Thrakell Dees.

Thrakell could be a valuable confederate. Could be. She wasn't sure what else he might be. Neto suspected he was a murderer, that he'd done away with other circuit survivors. There was no proof of it, but Telzey hadn't taken her attention off him since she'd caught him stalking her in his uncanny manner on the gallery, and there'd been an occasional shimmer of human thought through the cover pattern, which he'd changed meanwhile to that of a Fossily mechanic. She'd made out nothing clearly, but what she seemed to sense at those moments hadn't reduced her uneasiness about Thrakell.

"Thrakell," she said, "before we get down to business, I'm giving you a choice."

He frowned. "A choice?"

"Yes. What I'd like you to do is to give up that Fossily cover and open your screens for a minute, so I can see what you're thinking. That would be simplest."

Thrakell shook his head. "I don't understand."

Neto chuckled softly.

"Oh, you understand," Telzey said. "You wanted to come along when I try to get out of the circuit, so you are coming along. But we didn't get off to a good start, and I don't feel I can take you on trust now. You could prove I can by letting me look at your mind. Just the surface stuff—I want to know what made you decide to contact me, that's all."

Thrakell's small eyes glittered with angry apprehension. But his voice was even. "What if I refuse?"

"Then Essu will take your weapons and circuit key pack."

Thrakell looked shocked. "That's completely unfair! If we became separated, I'd be confined to whatever section I happened to be in. I'd be helpless!"

"Well, that will make you see to it we *don't* get separated," Telzey said. "I don't think we should now. Which will it be?"

Thrakell jerked his head sullenly at Neto. "What about her?"

"She's sure of me," Neto told him. "Quite, quite sure! She's already been all through my mind, that's why!" She laughed.

Essu, round white eyes fixed on Thrakell, reached for a gun on his belt, and Thrakell said hastily, "Let the Tolant have the articles then! I rarely use a weapon, in any case. I detest violence."

Essu began going over him with his search devices. Telzey and Neto looked on.

Telzey could, in fact, be very sure of Neto. Neto had known no hope of escape from the circuit. She'd lived by careful planning and constant alertness for the past two years, a vengeful, desperate ghost slipping about the fringe areas which would open to the portal keys she'd obtained, as wary of the few wild humans who'd still been around at first as of the Elaigar and their alien servants. There were periods when she no longer believed there was a world outside the circuit and seemed unable to remember what she had done before she met the Elaigar. At other times, she was aware of what was happening to her and knew there could be only one end to that.

Then, once more trailing the murderer who could slip up on you invisibly if you weren't careful, trying to determine what sort of mischief he was involved in, she'd touched a new mind.

In moments, Neto knew something like adoration. She'd found a protector, and gave herself over willingly and completely. Let this other one decide what should happen now, let her take control, as she began doing at once.

Neto's stresses dissolved in blind trust. Telzey saw to it that they did.

"Two problems," Telzey remarked presently. "The diagrams don't show exits to Tinokti, and they seem to add up to an incomplete map anyway. Then the keys we have between us apparently won't let us into more than about a fourth of the areas that look worth checking out. We could be one portal step away from an exit, know it's there, and still not be able to reach it."

Thrakell said sourly, "I see no way to remedy that! Many sections have a specialized or secret use, and only certain Elaigar leaders have access to them. That might well be the case with sections containing planetary exits. Then there's the fact that the Alatta intruders have altered the portal patterns of large complexes. I'm beginning to suspect you'll find yourself no more able to leave the circuit than we've been!" He glanced briefly over at Neto.

"Well," Telzey said, "let's try to get the second problem worked out first. Essu knows where he can get pretty complete sets of portal packs. But he will need help."

"What place is that?" asked Thrakell suspiciously. "As far as I know, only the Suan Uwin possess omnipacks."

"That's what Essu thinks. These are in a safe in one of Stiltik's offices. He can open the safe."

Thrakell shook his head.

"Impossible! Suicidal! The headquarters of the Suan Uwin are closely guarded against moves by political enemies. Even if we could get into Stiltik's compound, we'd never get out again alive!"

Neto said boredly to Telzey, "Why don't you lock this thing up somewhere? We can pick him up afterwards, if you feel like taking him along."

That ended Thrakell's protests. It wasn't, in fact, an impossible undertaking. Stiltik used Essu regularly to carry out special assignments which she preferred not to entrust even to close followers. There was a portal, unmarked and unguarded, to which only she and the Tolant had a key. If they were careful, they could get into the headquarters compound.

They did presently. They were then in a small room behind a locked door. To that door again only Stiltik and Essu had keys. Unless Stiltik happened to come in while they were there, they should be safe from detection.

Telzey scanned while her companions remained behind cover. It took time because she went about it very carefully, touching minds here and there with gossamer lightness. Details gradually developed. At last she thought she'd gathered a sufficiently complete picture.

Elaigar minds were about—some two dozen. There was no trace of Stiltik. The Suan Uwin appeared to be in an interrogation complex with the captured Alatta; and that understandably was a psi-blocked unit. There were Tolant minds and two unfamiliar alien mind types here. The serfs didn't count, and the only Elaigar in the central offices were two bored Otessan females, keeping an eye on the working staff. They might notice Essu going into Stiltik's offices presently, but there was nothing unusual about that. They weren't likely to be aware he was supposed to be somewhere else.

Another of the minds around here might count for a great deal. It was that of Stiltik's dagen.

The work she'd put in improving her psi techniques with Sams Larking and by herself was making all the difference now, Telzey thought. When Bozo was tracking her, she'd felt and been nearly helpless. She'd better remain very wary around this psi beast, but she wasn't in the least helpless, and knew it. Her screens hid her mind from it, and she'd learned how to reach through the screens with delicately sensing probes.

A probe reached toward the dagen mind—the barest touch. There was no reaction. Cautiously then, Telzey began to trace out what she could discern.

The creature was in an enclosure without physical exits. It needed none, of course. On Stiltik's order, it could flick itself into the enclosure and out again.

It could do very little that wasn't done on Stiltik's mental orders. Stiltik had clamped heavy and rigid controls on her monster. A human mind placed under similar controls would have been effectively paralyzed. The dagen's rugged psyche was in no sense paralyzed. It simply was unable to act except as its handler permitted it to act.

It wasn't very intelligent, but it knew who kept it chained.

Telzey studied the controls until she was satisfied she understood them. Then she told Essu to go after the omnipacks in Stiltik's office. She accompanied him mentally, alert for developing problems. Essu encountered none and was back with the packs five minutes later. He'd been seen but disregarded. Nothing seemed to have changed in the headquarters compound.

They left by the secret portal, and Essu handed Telzey its key. She said to the others, "Wait for me here! When I come out, we'll go back along the route we came—and for the first few sections we'll be running."

Thrakell Dees whispered agitatedly, "What are—"

She stepped through the portal into the room. Her mind returned gently to the dagen mind. The beast seemed half asleep now.

Psi sheared abruptly through Stiltik's control patterns. As abruptly, the dagen came awake. Telzey slipped out through the portal.

"Now *run!*"

Essu's haul of portal key packs had been eminently satisfactory. One of them had been taken from Tscharen after his capture. Essu interlocked it with an omnipack, gave the combination to Telzey. She slipped it into a pocket of the Fossily suit. It was small, weighed half as much as Essu's gun which was in another pocket of the suit. But it would open most of the significant sections of the circuit to her. Essu assembled a duplicate for himself with a copy of Tscharen's pack, clamped the other keys together at random, and pocketed both sets.

Thrakell Dees looked bitter, but said nothing. The arrangement was that he would stay close enough to Essu to pass through any portal they came to with the Tolant. Neto would stay similarly close to Telzey.

"And now?" Thrakell asked.

"Now we'll pick a route to the hospital area where the Tanvens put me back in shape," Telzey said. "We still want a guide."

15

The Third Planetary Exit control room was quiet. Telzey was at the instrument stand, watching the viewscreen. Thrakell Dees sat on the floor off to her left, with his back to the wall. He was getting some of her attention. A Sattaram giant was near the door behind her. He needed no attention—he was lying on his back and very dead.

In a room on the level below them, Neto and Korm, one-time Suan Uwin of the Elaigar, waited behind a locked door. Some attention from Telzey was required there from moment to moment, mainly to make sure Korm kept his mind shield tight. He'd been out of practice too long in that matter. Otherwise, he seemed ready to go. Neto was completely ready to go.

The viewscreen showed the circuit exit area on the other side of the locked door. The portal which opened on Tinokti was within a shielded vaultlike recess of a massive square structure a hundred yards across—mainly, it seemed, as a precaution against an Alatta attempt to invade the circuit at this point. The controls of the shielding and of the portal itself were on the instrument stand, and Telzey was ready to use them. She was also ready to unlock the door for Neto and Korm.

135

She couldn't do it at the moment. Something like a dozen Elaigar stood or moved around the exit structure. They were never all in sight at the same time, so she wasn't sure of the number. It was approximately a dozen. Most of them were Otessans; but at least three Sattarams were among them. Technically, they were on guard duty. Telzey had gathered from occasional washes of Elaigar thought that the duty was chiefly a disciplinary measure; these were members of visiting teams who'd got into trouble in the circuit. They weren't taking the assignment very seriously, but all wore guns. About half of them might be in view along the front of the structure at any one time. At present, only four were there.

Four were still too many. Essu would have been useful now, but Essu was dead. Korm had been leading them through a section like a giant greenhouse, long untended, when they spotted a Boragost patrol coming toward them and realized an encounter couldn't be avoided. The troops handled it well. Telzey and Thrakell didn't take part in the action, and weren't needed. The patrol—a Sattaram, an Otessan, six or seven Tolants— was ambushed in dense vegetation, wiped out in moments. Korm gained a Sattaram uniform in Boragost's black and silver, which was better cover for him than what he was wearing. And Telzey lost Essu.

She spared a momentary glance for Thrakell Dees. He was watching her, face expressionless.

When they'd taken the control room, looked at the situation in the exit area, she'd said to him, "You realize we can only get Neto through here. You and I'll have to get away and do something else."

Korm wouldn't accompany them—that was understood by everyone in the room but Korm.

Thrakell hadn't argued, and Telzey wasn't surprised.

She'd been studying him as she'd studied Korm on the way, trying to draw in as much last-minute information on a number of matters as she could. It had seemed to her presently that Thrakell Dees didn't really intend to leave the Elaigar circuit. Why he'd approached her originally remained unclear. What he mainly wanted now was one of the portal omnipacks she carried, the one Essu had assembled for her, or the one she'd taken from Essu after he was killed.

Thrakell had mentioned it, as a practical matter, after Korm and Neto took up their stations on the lower level, and they were alone in the control room.

"Thrakell," she'd said, "I need *you* as a guide now. There's a place I want to go to next, and it seems to be about as far from this part of the circuit as one can get. I might find it by myself with the maps, but it'll be faster with you. We've already spent too much time. I want to be there before anyone starts hunting for me."

Thrakell blinked slowly.

"What's the significance of the place?"

"The Alattas switched me into the circuit by a portal," Telzey said. "It may still be there and operational. If it is, you can get back to Tinokti, if you like. Or you can have one of the omnipacks—after you've let me look into your mind. That's still a condition. We can split up at that point. Not yet."

Thrakell stared at her a moment.

"I had the curious impression," he remarked, "that you'd decided before we got here you wouldn't be using this exit yourself to leave the circuit. The degree of control you've been exercising over Korm and Neto Nayne-Mel shows you could have arranged to do it, of course. I'm wondering about your motivation."

She smiled. "That makes us even. I've wondered a bit about yours."

But it had startled her. So he'd been studying her, too. She'd tried to be careful, but tensions were heavy now and she'd been preoccupied. She wasn't sure how much she might have revealed.

It was true she couldn't afford to leave yet. There were possibilities in the overall situation no one could have suspected, and her information wasn't definite enough. A faulty or incomplete report might do more harm than none; she simply wasn't sure. Through Neto she could see to it that the Service would at least know everything she was able to guess at present. So Neto would be maneuvered safely out of the circuit here. If possible.

But Neto wouldn't report immediately. The planetary exit opened into an old unused Phon villa. Neto would find money and aircars there. She'd get out of her Fossily disguise, move on and lie low in one of Tinokti's cities for the next ten days. If Telzey hadn't showed up by that time, Neto would contact the Psychology Service.

Telzey leaned forward suddenly, hands shifting toward the controls she'd marked. Thrakell stirred in his corner.

"Stay where you are!" she told him, without taking her eyes from the screen. Essu's gun lay on the stand beside her. With neither Essu nor Neto to watch him, Thrakell was going to take careful handling.

She nudged Neto, Korm. *Alert!* Neto responded. Korm didn't. He hadn't felt the nudge consciously, but he was now aware that the action might be about to begin. He was eager for it. Telzey had spent forty minutes working on him before he led them out of the hospital area. It was a patchwork job, but it would hold up as long as it had to. Korm's fears and hesitancies had been blocked away; in his mind, he was the lordly Suan Uwin of a few years ago. Insult had been offered him, and there was a raging thirst for vengeance simmering just below the surface, ready to be triggered. His great knife hung from his belt along with two Elaigar guns.

Two of the four Otessans who'd been in view in the screen still stood near the shielded portal recess. The other pair had moved toward the corner of the structure, and a Sattaram now had appeared there and was speaking to them. Telzey's finger rested on the door's lock switch. She watched the three, biting her lip.

The Sattaram turned, went around the side of the structure. The two Otessans followed. As they vanished, she unlocked the door in the room below. Whisper of acknowledgement from Neto.

And now to keep Korm's shield tight—tight—

He came into view below. The two remaining Otessans turned to look at him. He strode toward them, the fake Fossily mechanic trotting nimbly at his heels, keeping Korm between herself and the Otessans. Korm was huge, even among Sattarams. He was in the uniform of an officer of Boragost's command, and his age-ravaged face was half hidden by black rank markings which identified him as one of Boragost's temporary deputies. The two might be curious about what special duty brought him here, but no more than that.

He came up to them. His knife was abruptly deep in an Otessan chest.

They had flash reactions. The other had leaped sideways and back, and his gun was in his hand. It wasn't Korm but the gun already waiting in Neto's hand which brought that one down. She darted past him as the recess shield opened and the exit portal woke into gleaming life behind it. Through recess and portal—gone! The recess shield closed.

Korm's guns and his fury erupted together. Turning from the screen, Telzey had a glimpse of Elaigar shapes appearing at the side of the structure, of two or three

going down. Korm roared in savage triumph. He
wouldn't last long, but she'd locked the door on the lower level again. Survivors couldn't get out until someone
came to let them out. . . .

That, however, might happen at any time.

She was seen twice on the way to the brightly lit big
room where she and Tscharen had been captured, but
nobody paid the purposefully moving mechanic any attention; and, of course, nobody saw Thrakell Dees. Another time they spotted an approaching Fossily work
party led by a pair of Otessans, and got out of sight.
They had to stay out of sight a while then—the mechanics were busy not at all far from their hiding place.
Telzey drifted mentally about the Otessans, presently
was following much of their talk.

There were interesting rumors going around about the
accident in the headquarters compound of Stiltik's command. The two had heard different versions. It was clear
that the Suan Uwin's mind hound had slipped its controls and made a shambles of the place. Stiltik's careless-
ness . . . or could wily old Boragost have had a hand in
that slipping? They argued the point. The mind hound
was dead; so were an unspecified number of Stiltik's top
officers. Neither fact would *hurt* Boragost! But how
could he have gone about it?

Stiltik, unfortunately, wasn't among the casualities.
She'd killed the dagen herself. Telzey thought it might at
least keep her mind off the human psi for a while,
though that wasn't certain. The ambushed Boragost patrol apparently hadn't been missed yet; nor was there
mention of a maniac Sattaram who'd tried to wipe out
the guards at Planetary Exit Three. The circuit should be
simmering with rumors and speculations presently.

They reached the big room at last. Telzey motioned

Thrakell to stand off to one side, then went toward the paneled wall through which she'd stepped with Tscharen, trying to remember the exact location of the portal. Not far from the center line of the room. . . . She came to that point, and no dim portal outline appeared in the wall. She turned right, moved along the wall, left hand sliding across the panels. Eight steps on, her hand dipped into the wall. Now the portal was there in ghostly semivisibility.

She turned, beckoned to Thrakell Dees.

She'd memorized the route along which Tscharen had taken her, almost automatically, but thinking even then it wasn't impossible she'd be returning over it by herself. She found now she had very little searching to do. It helped that these were small circuit sections, a few rooms cut here and there out of Tinokti's buildings. It helped, too, that Thrakell remained on his best behavior. When they passed through the glimmering of a portal into another dim hall or room, he was closer to her than she liked, but that couldn't be avoided. Essu's gun was in a pocket on the side she kept turned away from him. Between portals he walked ahead of her without waiting to be told.

He knew they'd entered a sealed area and should know they were getting close to the place where she'd been brought into the circuit. Neither of them mentioned it. Telzey felt sure he didn't have the slightest intention of letting her look into his mind, couldn't afford to do it. What he did intend beyond getting one of the key packs remained obscure. Not a trickle of comprehensible thought had come through the blur of reproduced alien patterns, which now seemed to change from moment to moment as if Thrakell were mimicking first one species, then another. He might be trying to distract her. She had no further need of him as a guide;

in fact, he soon could become a liability. The question was what to do with him.

She located the eight portals along the route in twice as many minutes. Then, at the end of a passage, there was a door. She motioned Thrakell aside again, tried the handle, drew the door back, and was looking down one side of the ell-shaped room into which she'd been transported from the Luerral Circuit. The other door, the one by which the three Alattas had entered, stood open. The big wall closet they'd used for storage was also open. A stink of burned materials came from it. So Stiltik's searchers had been here.

She glanced at Thrakell. His intent little eyes met hers for an instant. She indicated the room. "Stand over there against the wall! I want to look around. And keep quiet—Stiltik had gadgets installed here. They just might still be operating."

He nodded, entered the room and stopped by the wall. Telzey went past him, to the corner of the ell. There were no signs of damage in the other part of the room. The portal which had brought her into the circuit might still be there, undetected, and one of the keys Tscharen had carried might activate it.

She'd wanted to find out about that. In an emergency, it could be the last remaining way of escape.

There was an abrupt crashing sound high above her, to her left. Startled, she spun around, looking up.

Something whipped about her ankles and drew her legs together in a sudden violent jerk, throwing her off balance.

16

She went down, turning, as the metal ring Thrakell had pitched against the overhead window strip to deflect her attention clattered to the floor. The Fossily bag on her back padded her fall. Thrakell, plunging toward her, came to an abrupt stop five feet away.

"You almost made it!" Telzey said softly. "But don't you dare move now!"

He looked at the gun pointed at his middle. His face whitened. "I meant no harm! I—"

"Don't talk either, Thrakell. You know I may have to kill you. So be careful!"

Thrakell was silent then. Telzey got into a sitting position, drew her legs up, looked at her ankles and back at Thrakell. The thing that clamped her legs together, held them locked tightly enough to be painful, was the round white cord which had been wrapped about his waist as a belt. No belt—a weapon, and one which had fooled Essu and his search instruments.

"How do you make it stop squeezing and come loose?" she asked.

It seemed there were controls installed in each tapered end of the slick white rope. Telzey told Thrakell to get down on hands and knees, stretched her legs out toward

143

him, and had him crawl up until he could reach her ankles and free her. Then she edged back, got to her feet. The gun had remained pointed at Thrakell throughout. "Show me how to work it," she said.

Thrakell looked glum, but showed her. It was simple enough. Hold the thing by one end, press the setting that prepared it to coil with the degree of force desired. Whatever it touched next was instantly wrapped up.

Telzey put the information to use, and the device soon held Thrakell's wrists pinned together behind him.

"Now let me explain," he said. He cleared his throat. "I realized the circuit exit of which you spoke must be somewhere nearby—probably in this room. I was afraid you might have decided to use it and leave me here. I only wanted to be certain you didn't. Surely, you understand that?"

"Just stay where you are," Telzey said.

The key packs she carried evoked no portal glimmer anywhere in the big room. The one which had transported her here probably had been destructured immediately afterwards. So there'd be no emergency escape open to her now by that route. Part of one of the walls of the adjoining room had been blasted away, down to the point where its materials were turned into unyielding slickness by the force field net pressing against them.

Telzey looked at the spot a moment. There had been a portal there, the one by which the three Alattas had entered. But Stiltik's search party had located it, and made sure it wouldn't be used again. No other portal led away from the room.

She went back into the big room, told Thrakell, "Go stand against the wall over there, facing me."

"Why?" he said warily.

"Go ahead. We have to settle something."

Thrakell moved over to the wall with obvious reluctance. "You haven't accepted my explanation?"

"No," Telzey said.

"If I'd wanted to hurt you, I could have set the cord as easily to break your legs!"

"Or my neck," Telzey agreed. "I know you weren't trying to do that. But I have to find out what you were trying to do. So get rid of that blur over your mind, and open your screens."

"I'm afraid that's impossible," Thrakell said.

"You won't do it?"

"I'm unable to do it. I can dispel one pattern only by forming another." Thrakell shrugged, smiled. "I have no psi screen otherwise, and my mind evidently refuses to expose itself! I can do nothing about it consciously."

"That's about what I told Stiltik when she wanted me to open my screens," Telzey said thoughtfully. "She didn't believe me. I don't believe you either." She took Essu's gun from her pocket.

Thrakell looked at the gun, at her face. He shook his head.

"No," he said. "You might have killed me after I tripped you up. You felt threatened. But you won't kill someone who's helpless and can't endanger you."

"Don't count on it," Telzey said. "Right now, I'll be trying not to kill you—but I probably will, anyway."

Alarm showed in Thrakell's face. "What do you mean?"

"I'm going to shoot as close to you as I can without hitting you," Telzey explained. "But I'm not really that good a shot. Sooner or later, you'll get hit."

"That's—"

She lifted the gun, pointed it, pressed the trigger button. There was a thudding sound, and a blazing patch twice the size of her palm appeared on the wall four inches from Thrakell's left ear. He cried out in fright, jerked away from it.

Telzey said, somewhat shakily, "That wasn't where I was aiming! And you'd better not move again because I'll be shooting on both sides . . . like this!"

She didn't come quite as close to him this time, but Thrakell yelled and dropped to his knees.

"Above your head!" Telzey told him.

The concealing blur of mind patterns vanished. Thrakell was making harsh sobbing noises. Telzey placed the gun back in her pocket. Her hands were trembling. She drew in a slow breath.

"Keep it open," she said.

Presently, she added, "I've got what I wanted—and I see you're somebody I can't control. You can blur up again. And stand up. We're leaving. How long have you been working for Boragost?"

Thrakell swallowed. "Two years. I had no choice. I faced torture and death!"

"I saw that," Telzey said. "Come along."

She led the way from the room toward the portaled sections. She'd seen more than that. Thrakell Dees, as she'd suspected, hadn't joined her with the intention of getting out of the Elaigar circuit. He couldn't afford being investigated on Tinokti, particularly not by the Psychology Service; and if the Service learned about him from Neto or Telzey, he'd have no chance of avoiding an investigation. Besides, he'd made a rather good thing out of being a secret operator for Boragost. As he judged it, the Elaigar would remain securely entrenched on Tinokti and elsewhere in the Hub for a considerable time. There was no immediate reason to think of changing his way of life. However, he should be prepared to shift allegiance in case the showdown between Boragost and Stiltik left Stiltik on top, as it probably would. The return of Telzey alive was an offering which would smooth his way wih Stiltik. He'd hoped to be able to add to it the report of an undiscovered portal used by Alattas.

Under its blurring patterns, Thrakell's mind was wide open and unprotected. But Telzey couldn't simply take control of him as she'd intended. She'd heard there were psi minds like that. Thrakell's was the first she'd encountered. There seemed to be none of the standard control points by which a mind could be secured, and she didn't have time for experimentation. Boragost hadn't found a way to control Thrakell directly. It wasn't likely she would.

She said over her shoulder, "I'm taking you along because the only other thing I can do at the moment is kill you, and I'd still rather not. Don't ask questions—I'm not telling you anything. You'll just be there. Don't interfere or try to get away! If I shoot at you again, I won't be trying to miss."

There were portals in the string of sections she'd come through which led deeper into the circuit's sealed areas. At least, there had to be one such portal. The three Alattas had used it in effecting their withdrawal; so had Stiltik's hunters in following them. It should open to one of the keys that had been part of Tscharen's pack.

Telzey found the portal in the second section up from the big room, passed through it with Thrakell Dees into another nondescript place, dingy and windowless. A portal presently awoke to glimmering life in one of the walls. They went on.

The next section was very dimly lit and apparently extensive. Telzey stationed Thrakell in the main passage, went into a room, checked it and an adjoining room out, returned to the passage, started along it—

Slight creak of the neglected flooring—and abrupt blazing awareness of something overlooked. She dropped to her knees, bent forward, clawing out Essu's gun.

Thrakell's strangle rope slapped against the passage wall above her. She rolled away from it as it fell, and Thrakell pounced on her, pinning her to the floor on her side, the gun beneath her. She forced it out, twisted the muzzle up, pressed the trigger blindly. There was the thudding sound of the charge, and a yell of alarm from Thrakell. Something ripped at the Fossily suit. Then his weight was abruptly off her. She rolled over, saw him darting along the passage toward the portal through which they'd come, knew he'd got one or both of her key packs.

She pointed the gun at the moving figure, pressed the trigger five or six times as quickly as she could. She missed Thrakell. But the charges formed a sudden blazing pattern on the portal wall ahead of him, and he veered aside out of the line of fire and vanished through a doorspace that opened on the passage.

Breathing hard, Telzey came up on her knees, saw one of the key packs lying beside her, picked it up, looked at it and put it in her left suit pocket. The pocket on the right side had been almost torn off, and Thrakell had got away with the other pack. Something stirred behind her. She glanced around, saw the white rope lying against the wall a few feet away—stretched out, shifting, turning with stiff springy motions, unable to grip what it had touched. She stood up on shaky legs, reached down until the gun almost touched the thing, and blasted it apart. Thrakell wasn't going to be able to use that device against her again—this time it *had* been aimed at her neck.

She started quietly down the passage toward the doorspace, gun held ready to fire. No sounds came from anywhere in the section, and she could pick up no trace of Thrakell's camouflage patterns. She didn't like that—she wasn't sure now he mightn't have tricks he hadn't revealed so far.

She stepped out before the doorspace, gun pointing into the room behind it.

It was a rather small room, as dimly lit as the rest of the section, and empty. Not-there effect or not, Thrakell wasn't in it; after a moment, Telzey felt sure of that. There was another doorway on one side. She couldn't see what lay beyond it. But if it was a dead end, if it didn't lead to a portal, she had Thrakell boxed in.

She started cautiously into the room.

Her foot went on down through the floor as if nothing were there. She caught at the doorjamb with her free hand, discovered it had become as insubstantial as the floor. Falling, she twisted backward, landed on her back in the passage, legs dangling from the knees down through the nothingness of the room's floor . . . through a portal.

She discovered then that she'd hung on to the gun. She let go of it, squirmed back from the trap, completely unnerved.

17

No need to look farther for Thrakell Dees! When Telzey felt steady enough to stand up, she went back to the two rooms she'd checked. A partly disassembled piece of machinery stood in one of them. She looked it over, discovered a twelve foot section of thin, light piping she could remove, detached it and straightened it out. She took that to the room with the portal flooring, reached down through the portal with it. The tip didn't touch anything even when she knelt in the doorway, her hand a few inches above the floor, and when she twisted the piping about horizontally, she didn't reach the sides of whatever was below there either.

She drew the piping out again. It was cold to the touch now, showed spots of frosting. The portal trap extended about twelve feet into the room. It had been activated by her key pack, as it had been activated by the pack Thrakell had taken from her. Wherever he'd gone, he wasn't likely to be back.

Essu and Thrakell had heard that the group Stiltik sent into the sealed areas after the Alattas had run into difficulties and returned. If this was a sample of the difficulties they'd run into, it wasn't surprising that Stiltik seemed to have been in no great hurry to continue to dig the three out of hiding.

When Telzey started off again to look for the portal which would take her on to the next section, her key pack was fastened to the tip of the piping, and she didn't put her foot anywhere the pack hadn't touched and found solid first. Her diagram maps didn't tell her at all definitely where she was, but did indicate that she'd moved beyond the possibility of being picked up in scanning systems installed by Stiltik's technicians. What lay ahead was, temporarily at least, Alatta territory. And the Alattas had set up their own scan systems. Presently she should be registering in them.

She uncovered a number of other portal traps. One of them, rather shockingly, was a wall portal indistinguishable from all the others she'd passed through. If she hadn't been put on guard, there would have been no reason to assume it wasn't the section exit she was trying to find. But a probe with the piping revealed there was a sheer drop from beyond. The actual exit was a few yards farther on along the wall. She passed through a few larger sections of the type she'd had in mind as a place to get rid of Thrakell Dees, stocked with provisions sufficient to have kept him going for years, or until someone came to get him out. She stopped in one of them long enough to wash the Fossily tiger striping from her face.

And then she was in a section where it seemed she couldn't go on. She'd been around the walls and come back to the portal by which she'd entered. She stood still, reflecting. She'd expected to reach a place like this eventually. What it would mean was that she had come to the limit of the area made open to Tscharen's portal keys. There should be a second portal here—one newly provided with settings which could be activated only by keys carried now by the other three Alattas.

But she hadn't expected to get to that point so soon.

Her gaze shifted to an area of flooring thirty feet away. There was a portal there. A trap. An invisible rectangle some eight feet long by six wide, lying almost against the wall. She'd discovered it as she moved along the wall, established its contours, gone around it.

She went back there now, tapping the floor ahead of her with the key pack until it sank out of sight. She drew it back, defined the outline of the portal with it again, moved up to the edge. She hadn't stopped to probe the trap before, there'd been no reason for it. Now she reversed the piping, gripped it by the pack, let the other end down through the portal.

There was a pull on the piping. She allowed it to follow the pull. It swung to her left as if drawn by a magnet on the far side of the portal, until its unseen tip touched a solid surface. It stayed there. Telzey's eyelids flickered. She moved quickly around to that end of the portal, knelt down beside it, already sure of what she'd found.

She pulled out the piping, reached through the portal with her arm, touched a smooth solid surface seemingly set at right angles to the one on which she knelt. She patted it probingly, lifted her hand away and let it drop back—pulled by gravity which also seemed set at right angles to the pull of gravity on this side of the portal. She shoved the piping through then, bent forward and came crawling out of the lower end of a wall portal into a new section.

Something like two hours after setting out from the big room with Thrakell Dees, she knew she'd reached the end of her route. She was now on the perimeter of the area the Alattas had made inaccessible to all others. She'd checked the section carefully. The only portal she could use here was the one by which she'd entered. Her key pack would take her no farther.

There was nothing to indicate what purpose this section originally had served. It was a sizable complex with a large central area, smaller rooms and passages along the sides. It was completely empty, a blank, lifeless place in which her footsteps raised hollow echoes. She laid the piping down by a wall of the central area, got her Tinokti street clothes out of the Fossily tool bag, changed to them, and sat down with her back to the wall.

A waiting game now. She leaned her head against the wall, closed her eyes. Mind screens thinned almost to the point of nonexistence, permitting ultimate sensitivity of perception. Meanwhile she rested physically.

Time passed. At last, her screens tightened in abrupt warning. She thinned them again, waited again.

Somewhere something stirred.

It was the least, most momentary of stirrings. As if ears had pricked quietly, or sharp eyes had turned to peer in her direction, not seeing her yet but aware there was something to be seen.

A thought touched her suddenly, like a thin cold whisper:

"If you move, make a sound, or think a warning, you'll die."

There was a shivering in the air. Then a great dagen crouched on the floor fifteen feet away, squatted back on its haunches, staring at Telzey. Swift electric thrills ran up and down her spine. This was a huge beast, bigger and heavier than the other two she'd seen, lighter in color. The small red eyes in the massive head had murder in them.

Her screens had locked instantly into a defensive shield. She made no physical motion at all.

The mind hound vanished.

Telzey's gaze shifted to the left. A tall figure stood in

a passage entrance, the Alatta woman Kolki Ming. For a moment, she studied Telzey, the Fossily bag, the length of piping with the attached key pack.

"This is a surprise!" she said. "We didn't expect you here, though there was some reason to believe you were no longer Stiltik's captive. You came alone?"

"Yes."

The Alatta nodded. "We'll see."

She remained silent a minute or two, eyes fixed expressionlessly on Telzey. Telzey guessed the dagen was scouting through adjoining sections.

Kolki Ming said suddenly, "It seems you did come alone. How did you escape?"

"Stiltik put a Tolant in charge of me. Essu. We were off by ourselves."

"And you took Essu under control?"

"Yes."

"Where is he now?"

"He got killed. We ran into some of Boragost's people."

"A patrol in the ninety-sixth sector?"

"A big greenhouse."

"You've been busy today!" Kolki Ming remarked. "That patrol was reported wiped out by gunfire. Tell me the rest of it."

Neto Nayne-Mel wouldn't be mentioned. Telzey gave a brief and fairly truthful account of her activities otherwise. She'd planned to get back to Tinokti at once, had realized by the time she reached the planetary exit why she couldn't—that she didn't know enough about the role the Alattas were playing in connection with the Tinokti circuit and in the Hub. She found then she'd worked Korm up too far to restrain him sufficiently. She and Thrakell Dees left for the sealed areas, while Korm went after the exit guards.

"Where is Boragost's strangler now?" the Alatta asked.

"We had a disagreement. He fell through one of your portal traps."

Kolki Ming shook her head slightly.

"And you're here to find out what we're doing," she said. "The Elaigar have one dagen less at their disposal, which is no small advantage to us. We might seem to owe you the information. But we can't let you take it to the Psychology Service. Essu's body, incidentally, wasn't found with the dead of the patrol."

"We took him along and hid him somewhere else," Telzey said. "I thought Stiltik mightn't know yet that I'd got away."

"She may not." The Alatta considered. "We're involved in an operation of extreme importance. Tscharen's capture has forced us to modify it and made it much more difficult than it should have been. It will have to be concluded quickly if it's to succeed. I'm not sure we can fit you in, but for the moment, at least, you're coming with me. Let me have your gun."

They emerged from a portal into a dark narrow street a few minutes later. The only light came from dim overhead globes. Looking back as they walked on, Telzey saw a dilapidated wall looming behind them. They'd stepped out of that. To right and left were small shabby houses, pressed close together. The cracked pavement was covered here and there by piles of litter. There was a stale smell in the air, and from somewhere arose a vague rumbling, so indistinct it seemed a tactile sensation rather than something heard.

"This section was some Phon's private experimental project," Kolki Ming said. "It doesn't appear on any regular circuit map and the Elaigar never found it, so we're using it as a temporary operations base." She glanced about. "Some two hundred people were trapped here when the Elaigar came. They escaped the general killing but were unable to leave the section and died when their supplies gave out."

She broke off. Something flicked abruptly through Telzey's awareness—a brief savage flash of psi. There was a gurgling howl, and the dagen materialized across the street from them.

"Scag was waiting for us, hoping to remain unnoticed," Kolki Ming said.

"He was going to attack?"

"If he got the chance. When he's under light working controls, as at present, he needs careful watching." They'd turned into another street, somewhat wider than the first, otherwise no different from it. On either side was the same ugly huddle of houses, light and silent. The mind hound was striding soundlessly along with them now, thirty feet away. The Alatta turned in toward one of the larger houses. "Here's my watchpost."

The ground floor of the house had been cleared of whatever it might have contained. Two portal outlines flickered on the walls, and a variety of instruments stood about, apparently hastily assembled. Kolki Ming said, "Ellorad and Sartes won't be back for a while. Sit down while I check on my duties."

"There's one thing I'd like to know," Telzey said.

"Yes?"

"How old are you?"

The Alatta glanced over at her.

"So you learned about that," she said. "I'm twenty-seven of your standard years. As for the rest of it, there may be time to talk later."

Telzey sat down on an empty instrument case, while Kolki Ming spoke briefly into a communicator. She seemed to listen then to a reply which remained in-audible to Telzey, and turned to a panel of scanning devices.

Presently they had time to talk.

The Elaigar's transition to the Sattaram form at maturity was connected with a death gene the Grisand cult on Nalakia had designed to help keep the mutation under control. The Elaigar didn't know it. After they destroyed the Grisands, they developed no biological science of their own, and to allow serf scientists to experiment physically with the masters was unthinkable under their code system.

But an early group had broken that rule. They set alien researchers the task of finding a method of prolonging their lives. They were told that for them as individuals there was no method, but that the gene could be deleted for their offspring. They settled for that—the Alattas came into existence. They remained Otessans in physical structure and had regained a normal human life span. With it, they presently regained lost interests and goals. They had time to learn, and learned very quickly because they could draw in the Elaigar manner on alien science and technology. Now they began making both their own.

Most of the Elaigar despised them equally for having abandoned the majestic structure of the mature Lion People and for degrading themselves with serf labor. They did their best to wipe out the new strain, but the Alattas drew ahead from the start.

"That was centuries ago, of course," said Kolki Ming. "We have our own civilization now and no longer need to borrow from others—though the Federation of the Hub was still one of our teachers on occasion as little as eighty years ago. The Elaigar remain dependent on their slave people and are no longer a match for us. And their codes limit them mentally. Some join us of their own accord, and while we can do nothing for them, their children acquire our life span. Otherwise, we collect the Elaigar at every opportunity, and whether they want it or not, any children of those we collect are also born as Alattas. They hate us for that, but they've become divided among themselves. In part, that's what led them to risk everything on this operation in the Hub. Bringing the old human enemy under control seemed a project great enough to unite them again. When we discovered what they were doing, we came back to the Federation ourselves."

Telzey said, "You've been trying to get them out of the Federation before we found out they were around?"

"That was the plan. We want no revival of that ancient trouble. It hasn't been a simple undertaking, but we've worked very carefully, and our preparations are complete. We three had the assignment to secure the central control section of the Tinokti circuit at a given moment. If we can get it now, most of the Sattaram leadership in the Hub will be trapped. We've waited months for the opportunity. We're prepared to move simultaneously against all other Elaigar positions in the Federation. So there's a great deal at stake. If we can't get the Elaigar out unnoticed before human forces contact them, it may become disastrous enough for all sides. To expect Federation warships to distinguish neatly between Alattas and Elaigar after the shooting begins would be expecting too much. And it would be no one-sided matter. We have heavy armament, as do the Elaigar."

She added, "The Elaigar are essentially our problem, not that of the Federation. We're still too close to them to regard them as enemies. My parents were of their kind and didn't elect to have their gene patterns modified. If they hadn't been captured and forced to it, I might have fought for Suan Uwin rank in my time as ruthlessly as Boragost or Stiltik—and, as I judge you now, so might you if your ancestors had happened to be Grisand research subjects on Nalakia. But we're gaining control of the Elaigar everywhere. If we succeed here, the last Sattaram will be dead less than thirty years from now."

She broke off, studied a set of indicators for a moment, picked up the communicator. Voice murmuring reached Telzey. It went on for perhaps two minutes. Kolki Ming set the communicator aside without replying. One of the other Alattas evidently had recorded a message for her.

She stood up, face thoughtful, fastened on a gun belt.

"We've been trying to force Boragost and Stiltik to open the Lion Game with us," she said. "It'll be the quickest way to accomplish our purpose. Perhaps the only way left at present! It seems we've succeeded." She indicated the street door. "We'll go outside. The first move should be made shortly. I must call in Scag."

Telzey came to her feet. "What's the Lion Game?"

"The one you're playing, I think," said Kolki Ming. "I don't believe you've been entirely candid with me. But whether it was your purpose or not, it seems you're involved in the Game now."

18

Kolki Ming had set up a light outside the house which brought full visibility to a hundred yard stretch of the dismal street and its house fronts. She and Telzey remained near the entrance. Scag now appeared abruptly in the illuminated area, stared coldly at them, glanced back bristling over his shoulder and was gone again.

Telzey had done the Alattas a greater favor than she knew in eliminating Stiltik's dagen. When they learned of it, they'd been able to go about their work more freely. A situation involving the possible use of dagens became so dangerously complicated that those threatened by them had to direct their primary efforts to getting the beasts out of the way. Scag had killed several of Stiltik's people during their surprise attack in the sealed areas; so it was known the three Alattas had brought a mind hound in with them.

There were two other dagens at present in the circuit, Boragost's and one whose handler was a Sattaram leader who had arrived with his beast during the week. Predictably, if Boragost was to take action against the Alattas, as it now seemed he would, his first step would be to use the pair to get rid of Scag. If the Elaigar dagens could be finished off at the same time, it would be worth the loss of Scag to the Alattas. They could go ahead immediately then with their plans.

That was the part of the game being played at present. Scag came and went. His kind could sense and track each other—he knew he was being sought by hunters as savage as he was. He wasn't trying to evade them. His role simply was to make sure the encounter took place here. The gun Kolki Ming held had been designed for use against dagens, who weren't easy creatures to kill.

Now Scag was back, and remained, half crouched, great head turning from side to side.

"They're coming!" Kolki Ming started forward. "Stay here and don't move!"

Abruptly, two other dagens appeared, to right and left of Scag. He hurled himself on the nearest one.

It became a wild blur of noise and motion. The street filled with the deep howling voices of the mind hounds, sounding like peals of insane laughter. They grappled and slashed, flicked in and out of sight, seeking advantage. Yellow blood smears began to appear on the paving behind them. Scag seemed not at all daunted by the fact that he was fighting two; they were lesser beasts, though one wasn't much smaller than he. For moments, it looked to Telzey as if he might kill them unaided. But he was getting help. Kolki Ming shifted this way and that about that spinning tangle, gun in sporadic action, perilously close to the struggle. But the dagens ignored her.

Then one of Scag's opponents lay on the paving, neck twisted back, unmoving. Scag and the other rolled, locked together, across the street toward Telzey; she watched yellow blood pumping from the side of Scag's neck and through his jaws. The Alatta followed, gun muzzle now almost touching the back of the other dagen. The beast jerked around toward her, jaws gaping. Scag came to his feet, stood swaying a moment, head lowered, made a gurgling noise, fell.

The other, braced up on its forelegs, paralyzed hindquarters dragging, was trying to reach Kolki Ming. She stepped aside from its lunge. The gun blazed again at its flank. It howled and vanished.

She waited perhaps a minute, gun half lifted. Then she lowered it, turned back to Telzey.

"Gone back to its handler!" She was breathing deeply but easily. "They won't use that one again! But they'll learn from its mind before they destroy it that Scag and the other are dead. Now the codes take over!"

Both in practice and theory, the maximum range of portal shift was considered definitely established. The security of the Elaigar circuits control center was based on that. Sections within potential shift range of the center were heavily guarded; a threat to them would bring overall defense systems into instant action.

Alatta scientists had managed to extend the shift range. For ordinary purposes the increase was insignificant. But here specifically, it could allow Alatta agents to bypass guarded sections and reach the control center without alerting defenders. The four agents planted in the center had set up a series of camouflaged portal contacts which led for the most part through sealed areas and ended at the center. The chief responsibility for this part of the operation had been Tscharen's.

After the work was completed, it became a matter of waiting for the next of the periodic gatherings of Elaigar leaders. Tscharen's duties as a member of Stiltik's staff kept him in the circuit; the other three were sent off presently on various assignments. Tscharen evidently decided to add to his security measures and was observed at it. As a result, he and Telzey were picked up by Stiltik when his associates returned to the circuit to carry out the planned operation, and the others were revealed as Alatta agents.

The original scheme had to be abandoned. Stiltik had forced Tscharen to face her in formal combat and outmatched him easily. That made him her personal captive; she could use any information she was able to wring from him to her own advantage. It wasn't an immediate threat; it should be many hours before she broke down his defenses. But the Elaigar in general had been alerted. A direct approach to the control center section would almost certainly be detected.

The Alattas decided to play on the tensions between the Suan Uwin, considerably heightened at the moment because no one was sure of the significance of the events for which Telzey and her group were responsible. Ellorad and Sartes, the other two agents, controlled a number of minds in Boragost's command. Through them, the feeling spread among both Boragost's supporters and opponents that since Stiltik had walked the Lion Way in allowing the captured Alatta his chance in ritual combat, Boragost could do no less. He must give personal challenge to the three trapped in the sealed areas—which in turn would draw Stiltik back into the matter.

"You *want* to fight those monsters?" Telzey had said, somewhat incredulously.

"I'd sooner not have to face either of them," said Kolki Ming. "Stiltik, in particular. But that won't be my part here. With Sartes and Ellorad openly committed, it will seem we've accepted defeat and are seeking combat death in preference to capture. That should draw the attention of the Elaigar temporarily off me and give me a chance to get to the control center unnoticed."

She added, "The fighting will be less uneven than you

think. Tscharen had no special combat skills, but we others were trained to be collectors of the Elaigar and are as practiced in the weapon types allowed under their codes as any of them. Boragost might prefer to hunt us down with a sufficient force of Elaigar and Tolants, but his prestige is at stake. He's issued his challenge by sending his dagens in against ours, and that part is now concluded, with neither side retaining an advantage. We'll accept the challenge shortly by showing ourselves. Boragost is bound then by the codes."

She'd cut an opening in the heel of one of Telzey's shoes and was assembling a miniature pack of portal keys to fit into it. Each of the Alattas carried such a concealed set, and, in case of accidents, a more obvious but less complete pack of standard size such as the one taken from Tscharen. That was what had enabled them to withdraw so quickly from Stiltik's initial attack.

Telzey said, "It was the Alattas who were watching me on Orado, wasn't it?"

"I was," said Kolki Ming.

"Why? After you switched me into the circuit, you said there were people who wanted to see me."

"There are. We haven't as much information as we want about the type of psis currently in the Federation. We've avoided contact with them here, and even the Elaigar have had the sense to keep away from the institutions of the Psychology Service. But some now believe that the power of the Psychology Service is based chiefly on its use of psi machines rather than on its members' ability as psis—in fact, that psis of the original human strain simply don't develop a degree of ability that can compare with our own. And that can become dangerous thinking. We have our fools, as you do. Some of them might begin to assume that the Federation could be challenged with impunity."

"You don't think so then?" Telzey said.

"I happen to know better. But we wanted to be able to establish the fact beyond question. I learned on Orado that a Sattaram handler had set his dagen on a prying human psi and that the dagen then had inexplicably disappeared. That psi seemed worth further study, particularly after I'd identified you and discovered you hadn't yet attained your physical maturity. There also seemed to be a connection between you and the Psychology Service. It was decided to pick you up for analysis by experts, if it could be done safely. Then the Tinokti matter came up and you transferred here. That gave me the opportunity to bring you into the circuit. We expected to conclude our operation quickly, and take you along."

She added, "A lifetime of exile among us wasn't planned for you. You'd have remained unconscious throughout most of the analysis and presently have found yourself on Orado again, with nothing of significance concerning us to relate. I don't know what the arrangement will be now, assuming we survive the next hour or two."

Ellorad and Sartes arrived soon afterwards. They'd been checking on developments through their mind contacts. Boragost had expressed doubts publicly that the Alatta agents would choose combat. However, if they did, he'd be pleased to meet them in the Hall of Challenge and add their heads to his minor trophies. Stiltik wouldn't involve herself until Boragost had fought at least once.

"Boragost will have a witness?" Kolki Ming asked.

"Yes. Lishon, the Adjutant, as usual," said Sartes. "Stiltik, also as usual, will fight without witness—a hunt in the Kaht Chasm."

Ellorad added, "Sartes will face Boragost. I'll be his

witness there. We don't want to bring Stiltik into it too quickly." He glanced at Telzey. "When we show ourselves, she may learn for the first time that she's lost her human captive and grow hungry for action. But a Chasm hunt can be extended, and I'll make it thoroughly extensive. You should have the time to do what's necessary."

Kolki Ming nodded. "Yes, I should."

"Then let's determine our route! When we're seen, we should be within a few minutes of the Hall of Challenge, then out of sight again until Sartes and I actually enter the Hall. That will leave Stiltik no time to interfere with the present arrangement."

When they set off, the Alattas wore the short-sleeved shirts, trunks and boots which had been concealed by their Sparan garments. Long knives hung from their belts next to guns. Combat under code conditions allowed only weapons depending on physical dexterity and strength, and the weapons of psi. Guns were worn by witnesses as a formal guarantee that the codes would be observed. Principals didn't carry them.

Ellorad and Sartes strode ahead, moving with relaxed ease. They looked formidable enough, and if, to Telzey, even those long powerful bodies appeared no real match for the Sattaram giants, they should know what they were attempting—which might be only to give Kolki Ming time to conclude the operation.

Boragost's technicians had been at work in fringe sections of the sealed areas they'd been able to penetrate, setting up a scanning system, Kolki Ming had followed their progress on her instruments. The route she'd outlined would take them through such a section. Telzey didn't know they'd reached it until a Sattaram voice abruptly addressed them in the Elaigar language. They stopped.

The deep harsh voice went on, speaking slowly and with emphasis. When it finished, Ellorad replied, then started toward the end of the section. The others followed; and as soon as they'd left the section, they moved quickly. Kolki Ming said to Telzey, "That was Boragost's witness. The challenge has been acknowledged by both sides, and we've been told to select the one who is to face Boragost first and have him come at once with his witness to the Hall. It's the situation we wanted!"

They hurried after the men, came after another three sections into a room where the two had turned on a viewscreen. The screen showed a wide hall with black and silver walls. Two Sattarams stood there unmoving. The one farthest from the screen wore a gun belt. The other balanced a huge axe on his shoulder.

"They entered just now," Ellorad said. "Sartes is pleased to see Boragost has selected the long axe. He thinks he can spin out that fight until the Suan Uwin is falling over his own feet!"

The two left immediately. Sartes had removed his gun, but Ellorad retained his.

19

Kolki Ming said, "That hall is only two portals from
here, but the Elaigar haven't been able to establish access to these sections. Boragost doesn't know we can see
him. We'll wait till the combat begins, then be off on our
route at once."

Telzey nodded mutely. Boragost looked almost as
huge as Korm and seemed to her to show no indications
of aging. The handle of the axe he held must be at least
five feet long.

Ellorad and Sartes appeared suddenly in the screen,
moving toward the center of the hall. Sartes walked
ahead; Ellorad followed a dozen steps behind him and
to the right. The two Sattarams stood motionless,
watching them. A third of the way down the hall, Sartes
and Ellorad stopped. Ellorad spoke briefly. Lishon
rumbled a reply. Then Sartes drew his knife, and
Boragost grinned, took the axe in both hands and
started unhurriedly forward—

Kolki Ming sucked in her breath, sprang back from
the screen, darted from the room. Telzey sprinted after
her, mind in a whirl, not quite sure of what she'd seen.
There'd been the plum-colored shapes of Tolants suddenly on either side of the great hall. Three, it seemed,

168

on each side—yes, six in all! As she saw them, each had an arm drawn back, was swinging it forward, down. They appeared to be holding short sticks. She'd had a blurred glimpse of Ellorad snatching his gun from its holster, then falling forward, of Sartes already on the floor—

Kolki Ming was thirty feet ahead of her, racing down a passage, then disappeared through a portal at the end. Telzey passed through the portal moments later, saw the Alatta had nearly doubled the distance between them, was holding her gun. Kolki Ming checked suddenly then, vanished through the wall on her right.

That portal brought Telzey out into the great hall they'd been watching.

There, Kolki Ming's gun snarled and snarled.

Lishon was on his side, kicking, bellowing. Boragost had dropped to hands and knees, his great head covered with blood, shaking it slowly as if dazed. Smaller plum-colored bodies lay and rolled here and there on the floor. Two still darted squealing along the right side of the hall. The gun found one, flung him twisting through the air. The other turned abruptly, disappeared through the wall—

Portals. The Tolant troop had received some signal, stepped simultaneously into the hall through a string of concealed portals lining its sides. . . .

Boragost collapsed forward on his face, lay still.

Kolki Ming glanced around at Telzey, eyes glaring from a dead-white face, then hurried past Boragost toward Lishon. Telzey ran after her, skirting Sartes on the floor, saw something small, black and bushy planted in Sartes's shoulder. . . . Throwing sticks, poisoned darts.

Kolki Ming's gun spoke again. Lishon roared, in pain or rage. The Alatta reached him, bent over him, straightened, and now his gun was in her other hand.

She thrust it under her belt, started back to Boragost, Telzey trailing her, stood looking down at the giant, prodded his ribs with her boot. "Dead," she said in a flat voice.

She looked about the hall, wiped the back of her hand across her forehead. "All dead but Lishon, who shares Boragost's dishonor, and a frightened Tolant. Now we wait. Not long, I think! The Tolant will run in his panic to the Elaigar." She glanced down at Telzey. "Tolant poison—our two died as they fell. Three darts in each. Boragost didn't like the look of the Lion Way today! If we hadn't been watching, his scheme would have worked. The Tolants and their darts would have been gone, the punctures covered by axe strokes. We—"

She broke off.

A wide flight of stairs rose up to the rear of the hall beyond the point where Lishon lay. It had appeared to end against a blank wall. Now a great slab in that wall was sliding sideways—an opening door linked to an opening portal. A storm of deep voices and furious emotion burst through it simultaneously; then, as the opening widened, the Elaigar poured through in a crowd. The ones in the front ranks checked as they caught sight of Kolki Ming and Telzey and turned, outbellowing the others. The motion slowed; abruptly there was silence.

Kolki Ming, eyes blazing, flung up her arms, knife in one hand, gun in the other, shouted a dozen words at them.

One of the Sattarams roared back, tossing his head. The pack poured down the steps into the hall. The first to reach Sartes's body bent, plucked the dart from Sartes's shoulder, another from his side, held them up.

At that, there was stillness again. The faces showed shocked fury. The Sattaram who had replied to Kolki Ming growled something. A minor disturbance in the dense ranks followed. An Otessan emerged, holding a Tolant by the neck. The Tolant began to squeal. The Elaigar lifted him, clamped the Tolant's ankles together in one hand, swung the squirming creature around and up in a long single-armed sweep, down again. The squeals stopped as the body slapped against the flooring and broke.

The Sattaram looked over at Lishon, rumbled again. Three others moved quickly toward Lishon. His eyes were wide and staring as two hauled him to his feet, held him upright by the arms. The third drew a short knife, shoved Lishon's chin back with the heel of his hand, sank the knife deep into Lishon's throat, drew it sideways.

Dead Boragost didn't feel it, but he got his throat cut next.

They were elsewhere then in a room, Kolki Ming and Telzey, with something more than a dozen Sattarams. They didn't appear to be exactly prisoners at present. Their key packs had been taken from them—the obvious ones—but Kolki Ming retained her weapons. The Elaigar codes were involved; and from the loud and heated exchange going on, it appeared the codes rarely had been called upon to deal with so complicated a situation. Shields were tight all around. Telzey could pick up no specific impressions, but the general trend of talk was obvious. Kolki Ming spoke incisively now and then. When she did, the giants listened—with black scowls, most of them; but they listened. She was an enemy, but her ancestors had been Elaigar, and she and her associates had shown they would abide by the codes. Whereupon a Suan Uwin of the Lion people, aided by his witness, shamefully broke the codes to avoid facing Alattas in combat!

A damnable state of affairs! There was much scratching of shaggy scalps. Then Kolki Ming spoke again, now at some length. The group began turning their heads to stare at Telzey, standing off by the wall with a Sattaram who seemed to have put himself in charge of her. This monster addressed Telzey when Kolki Ming stopped speaking.

"The Alatta," he rumbled, "says you're an agent of the Psychology Service. Is that true?"

Telzey looked up at him, startled by his fluent use of translingue. She reminded herself then that in spite of his appearance he might be barely older than she—could, not much more than a year ago, have been an Otessan moving about among the people of the Hub in something like Sparan disguise.

"Yes, it's true," she said carefully.

There was muttering among the others. Apparently more than a few knew translingue.

"The Alatta further says," Telzey's Sattaram resumed, "that it was you who turned Stiltik's dagen on her in the headquarters, that you also stole her omnipacks and made yourself mind master of her chief Tolant as well as of Korm Nyokee, the disgraced one. And that it was you and your slaves who drew Boragost's patrol into ambush and killed them. Finally, that you chose to restore to Korm Nyokee the honor he'd lost by letting him seek combat death. Are all these things true?"

"Yes."

"Ho!" His tangled eyebrows lifted. "You then joined the Alatta agents to help them against us?"

"Yes."

"Ho-ho!" The broad ogre face split in a slow grin. He dug at his chin with a thumb nail, staring down at her. Grunts came from the group where one of them was speaking, apparently repeating what had been said for nonlinguists. Telzey collected more stares. Her guard clamped a crushing hand on her shoulder.

"I've told them before this," he remarked, "that there are humans who must be called codeworthy!" His face darkened. "More so certainly than Boragost and Lishon! No one believes now that was the first treachery committed by those two." He shook his great head glumly. "These are sorry times!"

The general discussion had resumed meanwhile, soon grew as heated as before. One of the Sattarams abruptly left the room. Telzey's giant told her, "He's to find out what Stiltik wants, since she alone is now Suan Uwin. But whatever she wants, we are the chiefs who will determine what the codes demand."

The Elaigar who'd left came back shortly, made his report. More talk, Kolki Ming joining in. The guard said to Telzey, "Stiltik claims it's her right to have the Alatta who was of her command face her in the Kaht Chasm. It's agreed this is proper under the codes, and Kolki Ming has accepted. Stiltik also says, however, that you should be returned to her at once as her prisoner. I think she feels you've brought ridicule on her, as you have. This is now being discussed."

Telzey didn't reply. She felt chilled. The talk went on. Her Sattaram broke in several times, presently began to grin. One of the giants in the group addressed her in translingue.

"Is it your choice," he asked, "to face Stiltik in the Kaht Chasm beside the Alatta Kolki Ming?"

Telzey didn't hesitate. "Yes, it is."

He translated. Nods from the group. Telzey's Sattaram said something in their language. A few of them laughed. He said to Telzey, holding out his huge hand, "Give me your belt!"

She looked up at him, took off her jacket belt and gave it to him. He reached inside his vestlike upper garment, brought out a knife in a narrow metal sheath, fastened the sheath on the belt, handed the belt back. "You were Stiltik's prisoner and freed yourself fairly!" he rumbled. "I say you're codeworthy and have told them so. You won't face Stiltik in the Kaht Chasm unarmed!" His toothy grin reappeared. "Who knows? You may claim Suan Uwin rank among us before you're done!"

He translated that for the group. There was a roar of laughter. Telzey's giant laughed with the others, but then looked down at her and shook his head.

"No," he said. "Stiltik will eat your heart and that of Kolki Ming. But if we find then that you were able to redden your knife before it happened, I shall be pleased!"

20

The portal to which Kolki Ming and Telzey were taken let them out into a sloping mountain area. When Telzey glanced back, a sheer cliff towered behind them. Tinokti's sun shone through invisible circuit barriers overhead.

Kolki Ming turned toward a small building a hundred yards away. "Come quickly! Stiltik may not wait long before following."

Telzey hurried after her. Behind the building, the rock-studded slope curved down out of sight. Perhaps half a mile away was another steep cliff face. Dark narrow lines of trees climbed along it; some sections were covered by tangles of vines. The great wall curved in to left and right until it nearly met the mountain front out of which they'd stepped. On the right, at the point where the two rock masses came closest, water streamed through, dropping in long cascades toward the hidden floor of Kaht Chasm. Far to the left, the stream foamed away through another break in the mountains.

If water—

Telzey brushed the thought aside. Whatever applications of portal technology were involved, the fact that water appeared to flow freely through the force barriers about this vast section didn't mean there were possible exit or entry points there.

She followed Kolki Ming into the building. The interior was a single large room. Mountaineering equipment, geared to Elaigar proportions, hung from walls and posts. Ropes, clamps, hooks . . . Kolki Ming selected a coil of transparent rope, stripped hooks from it, attached it to her belt beside the long knife which was now her only weapon. Outside the building, she stooped, legs bent. "Up on my back; hang on! We want to put distance between ourselves and this place."

Telzey scrambled up, clamped her legs around the Alatta's waist, locked her hands on the tough shirt material. Kolki Ming started down the slope.

"This is an exercise area for general use when it isn't serving as Stiltik's hunting ground," she said. "As a rule, the Suan Uwin likes a long chase, but today she may be impatient. She's tireless, almost as fast as I am, twice as strong, and as skilled a fighter on the rocks as in the water below. The only exit is at the end of the Chasm near the foot of the falls, and it will open now only to Stiltik's key. Beyond it is her Hall of Triumph where the Elaigar will wait to see her display her new trophies to them."

The slope suddenly dropped off. Kolki Ming turned her face to the rock, climbed on down, using hands and feet and moving almost as quickly as before. Telzey tightened her grip. She'd done some rock work for sport, but that had been a different matter from this wild, swaying ride along what was turning into a precipitous cliff.

A minute or two later, Kolki Ming glanced sideways and down, said, "Hold on hard!" and pushed away from the rock. They dropped. Telzey clutched convulsively. The drop ended not much more than twelve feet below, almost without a jar. Kolki Ming went on along a path some three feet wide, leading around a curve of the cliff.

Telzey swallowed. "How will Stiltik find us?" she asked.

"By following our scent trail until she has us in sight. She's a mind hunter, too, so keep your screens locked." Kolki Ming's breathing still seemed relaxed and unhurried. "This may look like an uneven game to the Elaigar, but since there always was a chance I would have to face Stiltik here some day, I've made the Chasm my exercise area whenever I was in the circuit . . . and they don't know that of the three of us I was the dagen handler."

The rumble of rushing water was audible now, and growing louder. The stream must pass almost directly beneath them, some three hundred yards down. They moved into shadow. The path narrowed, narrowed further. There came a place where the Alatta turned sideways and edged along where Telzey could barely make out footholds, never seeming to give a thought to the long drop below. Very gradually, the path began to widen again as the curve of the cliff reversed itself, leading them back into sunlight. And presently back into shadow.

Then, as they rounded another bulge, Telzey saw a point ahead where the path forked, one arm leading up through a narrow crevice, the other descending along the cliff. An instant later, a thought tendril touched her screens, coldly alert, searching. It lingered, faded.

"Yes, Stiltik's in the Chasm," Kolki Ming said. "She'll be on our trail in moments."

She took the downward fork. It curved in and out, dipped steeply, rose again. Kolki Ming checked at an opening in the rock, a narrow high cave mouth. Dirt had collected within it, and cliff vines had taken root and grown, forming a tangle which almost filled the opening.

Kolki Ming glanced back, parted the tangle, edged inside. "You can get down."

Telzey slid to the ground, stood on unsteady legs, drew a long breath, "And now?" she asked.

"Now," said Kolki Ming, voice and face expressionless, "I leave you. Don't think of me. Wait here behind the vines. You'll see Stiltik coming long before she sees you. Then be ready to do whatever seems required."

She turned, moved back into the dimness of the cave, seemed to vanish behind a corner. Completely disconcerted for the moment, Telzey stared after her. There came faint sounds, a scraping, the clattering of a dislodged rock. Then silence.

Telzey went to the cave opening, looked back along the path that wound in and out along the curves of the cliff. Stiltik would be in sight on it minutes before she got this far—and surely she couldn't be very close yet! Telzey moved into the cave, came to the corner around which Kolki Ming had disappeared. Almost pitch-darkness there. After a dozen groping steps, she came to a stop. There was a rock before her. On either side, not much more than two and a half feet apart, was also rock. Water trickled slowly down the wall on the right, seeping into the dust about her shoes.

She looked up into darkness, reached on tiptoe, arms stretching, touched nothing. A draft moved past her face. So here the cave turned upward, became a narrow tunnel; and up that black hole Kolki Ming had gone. Telzey wondered whether she would be able to follow, stood a moment reflecting, then returned to the cave opening. She sat down where she could watch their trail, drew the vines into a thicker tangle before her. Pieces of rock lay around, and her hands went out, began gath-

ering them into a pile, while her eyes remained fastened
on the path.

On the path, presently, Stiltik appeared, coming
around a distant turn. Telzey's breath caught. Stiltik's
bulk looked misshapen and awkward at that range, but
she moved with swift assurance, like a creature born to
mountain heights, along a thread of shelf almost in-
discernible from the cave. She went out of sight behind
the thrust of the mountain, emerged again, closer.

Telzey let a trickle of fear escape through her screens,
then drew them into a tight shield. She saw Stiltik lift her
head without checking her stride. Thought probed alertly about, slid away. But not entirely. She sensed a waiting watchfulness now as Stiltik continued to vanish and
reappear along the winding path.

Presently Telzey could begin to distinguish the features of the heavy-jawed face. A short-handled double-
headed hatchet hung from Stiltik's belt, along with a
knife and a coil of rope. She came to the point where the
path forked, paused, measuring the branch which led up
through the crevice, stooped abruptly, half crouched,
bringing her head close to the ground, face shifting back
and forth, almost nosing the path like a dog. Telzey saw
the bunching of heavy back muscles through the material of the sleeveless shirt. For a moment, it seemed wholly
the posture of an animal. The giantess straightened,
again looked up along the crevice. Telzey's hand moved
forward. The pile of rocks she'd gathered rattled
through the vines to the path below the cave opening. A
brief hot gust of terror burst from the shield.

Stiltik's head turned. Then, swiftly, she started along
the path toward the cave.

Telzey sat still, breathing so shallow it might almost

have stopped. Stiltik's mouth hung open; her eyes stared, seeming to probe through the vines. Around a curve she came, loosening the hatchet at her belt, cold mind impulses searching.

A psi bolt slammed, hard, heavy, fast, jarring Telzey through her shield. It hadn't been directed at her.

Stiltik swayed on the path, gave a grunting exhalation of surprise, and something flicked down out of the air above her like a thin glassy snake. The looped end of Kolki Ming's rope dropped around her neck, jerked tight.

One of her great hands caught at the rope, the other struck up with the hatchet. But she was stumbling backward, being hauled off the path. Two minds slashed at each other, indistinguishable in fury. Then Stiltik's massive body plunged down along the side of the cliff with a clatter of rocks, dropped below Telzey's line of sight. The rope jerked tight again; there was a crack like the snapping of a thick tree branch. The end of the rope flicked down past the path, following the falling body. From above came a yell, savage and triumphant. From below, seconds later, came the sound of impact.

Abruptly, there was stillness. Telzey drew a deep, sighing breath, stood up, pushed her way out through the vine tangles to the cave opening. She waited there a minute or two. Then Kolki Ming, smeared with the dark slime of the winding tunnel through which she'd crept to the cliff top, came down along the crevice to the fork of the path, and turned back toward the cave.

They reached the floor of the Kaht Chasm presently, found Stiltik's broken body. Kolki Ming drew her knife and was busy for a time, while Telzey sat on a rock and looked up the Chasm to the point where the foaming stream tumbled through a narrow break in the mountain. She thought she could make out a pale shimmer on the rocks. It should be the Chasm's exit portal, not far from the falls, and not very far from them now. Tinokti's sun had moved beyond the crest of the cliff. All the lower part of the Chasm lay in deep shadow.

Then Kolki Ming finished, came to Telzey and held up dripping hands. "Blood of a Suan Uwin!" she said. "The Elaigar will see your knife reddened. I wonder if they'll be pleased! Didn't you know I sensed you draw Stiltik's attention toward you when her suspicions awoke? If you hadn't, I'm not at all sure the matter could have ended well for either of us." She drew the knife from Telzey's belt, ran fingers over blade, hilt and sheath, replaced the knife. A knuckle tilted Telzey's chin up; a hand smeared wetness across her face. "Don't be too dainty!" Kolki Ming told her. "They're to see you took a full share of their Suan Uwin's defeat."

They walked along the floor of the Chasm, beside the cold rush of water, toward the portal shimmer, Stiltik's blood painting them, Stiltik's severed head swinging by its hair from Kolki Ming's right hand. The portal brightened as they reached it, and they went through.

The Elaigar stood waiting, filling the long hall. They walked forward, toward those nearest the portal. The giants stared, jaws dropping. A rumble of voices began here and there, ended quickly. The Elaigar standing before them started to move aside, clearing the way. The motion spread, and a wide lane opened through the ranks as they came on. Beyond, Telzey saw a ramp leading to a raised section at the end of the hall. They reached the ramp, went up it, and at the top Kolki Ming turned. Telzey turned with her.

Below stood the Lion People, unmoving, silent, broad faces lifted and watching. Kolki Ming's arm swung far back, came forward. She hurled Stiltik's head back at them. It bounced and rolled along the ramp, black hair whipping about, blood spattering. It rolled on into the hall, the giants giving way before it. Then a roar of voices arose.

"This way!" said Kolki Ming.

They were at the mall, passed through a portal, the noise cutting off behind them.

"Now quickly!"

They ran. None of the sections they went through in the next minutes looked familiar to Telzey, but Kolki Ming didn't hesitate. Telzey realized suddenly they were back in the sealed areas again; the portals here were of the disguised variety. She was gasping for breath, vision blurring with exhaustion. The Alatta was setting a pace she couldn't possibly keep up with much longer.

Then they were in a room with a viewscreen stand in one corner. Here Kolki Ming stopped. "Get your breath back," she told Telzey. "One more move only, and we have time for that—though perhaps no more time than it takes Stiltik's blood to dry on us." She was activating the screen as she spoke, spinning dials. Stiltik's Hall of Triumph swam into view, with a burst of Elaigar voices. Churning groups of the giants filled the hall; more had come in since they left, and others were still arriving. Most of them appeared to be talking at once; and much of the talk seemed furious argument.

"Now they debate!" said Kolki Ming. "What do the codes demand? Whatever conclusion they come to, it will involve our death. That's necessary. But first they must decide how to kill us with honor—to us and themselves. Then they'll start asking where we've gone."

She turned away. Telzey watched the screen a moment longer, her breathing beginning to ease. When she looked around, Kolki Ming had opened a closet in the wall, was fastening a gun she'd taken from it to her belt. She removed two small flat slabs of plastic and metal from a closet shelf, closed the closet, laid the slabs on a table. She came back to the screen, dialed to another view.

"The control section," she said. "Our goal now!"

The control section was a large place. Telzey looked out at a curving wall crowded with instrument stands. On the right was a great black square in the wall—a blackness which seemed to draw the mind down into vast depths. "The Vingarran Gate," said Kolki Ming. Two Sattarams stood at one end of the section, watching the technicians. They wore guns. The technicians, perhaps two dozen in all, represented three life forms, two of which suggested the humanoid type, though no more so than Couse's people. The third was a lumpy disk covered with yellow scales and equipped with a variety of flexible limbs.

"Those two must die," Kolki Ming said, indicating the Sattarams. "They're controlled servants of the Suan Uwin, jointly conditioned by Boragost and Stiltik as safeguard against surprises by either. The instrument handlers are conditioned, too, but they'll be no problem." She switched off the screen. "Now come." She took the two slabs from the table.

There was no more running, though Kolki Ming still moved swiftly. Five sections on, she stopped before a blank wall. "There's a portal here, left incomplete to prevent discovery," she said. "The section's on one of the potential approaches to the control area, so it's inspected frequently and thoroughly. Now I'll close the field!"

She searched along the wall, placed one of the slabs carefully against it. It adhered. She opened the back of the slab, adjusted settings, pressed the cover shut. "Come through immediately behind me," she told Telzey. "And be very quiet! On these last fifty steps, things might still go wrong."

They came out into semidarkness, went down a flight of stairs. Below, Kolki Ming halted, head turned. Telzey listened from behind her. There were faint distant sounds, which might be voices but not Elaigar voices. After some moments they faded. Kolki Ming moved on silently, Telzey following.

The remaining slab went against a wall. Peering through the dark, Kolki Ming made final adjustments. She paused then, stepped back. Her face turned toward Telzey.

"We weren't able to test this one," she whispered. "When I close the last switch, it will trigger alarms—here, in an adjoining guarded section, and in the control area. Be ready!"

Her left hand reached out to the slab. Sound blared in the darkness about them, and Kolki Ming had vanished through the portal. Telzey followed at once.

The two Sattarams on guard had no chance. Kolki Ming had emerged from the wall behind them, gun blazing. By then, there were guns in their hands, too; but they died before they saw her. She ran past the bodies toward the technicians at the instrument banks, shouting Elaigar orders above the clanging alarm din in the air. The technicians didn't hesitate. For a moment, there was a wild scramble of variously shaped bodies at an exit at the far end of the big room. Then the last of them disappeared.

Kolki Ming was at the instrument stands, gun back in its holster, hands flicking about. Series of buttons stabbed down. Two massive switches above her swung over, snapped shut. The alarm signal ended.

In the sudden silence, she looked at Telzey who had followed her across the room.

"And now," she said, drawing a deep breath, "it's

done! Every section in the circuit has been sealed. No portal can open until it's released from this room. Wherever the Elaigar were a moment ago, there they'll stay." She smiled without mirth. "How they'll rage! But not for long. Now I'll reset the Vingarran, and the Gate will open and my people will come through to remove our captives from section after section, and take them and their servants to our transports."

She went to another instrument console, unlocked it, bent over it. Telzey stood watching. The Alatta's hand moved to a group of controls, hesitated. She frowned. The hand shifted uncertainly.

Kolki Ming stiffened. Her hand jerked toward the gun at her belt. The motion wasn't completed.

She straightened then, turned to stare at Telzey. And Telzey felt the Alatta's mind turning also, wonderingly, incredulously, seeking a way to escape the intangible web of holds that had fastened on it, and realizing there was no way—that it was unable now even to understand how it was held.

"You?" Kolki Ming said heavily at last. "How could—"

"When you killed Stiltik."

A mind blazingly open, telepathically vulnerable, powers and attention wholly committed. Only for instants; but in those instants, Telzey, waiting and watching, had flowed inside.

"I sensed nothing," Kolki Ming shook her head. "Of course—that was the first awareness you blocked."

"Yes," Telzey said. "It was. I had plenty of time afterwards for the rest of it."

The Alatta's eyes were bleak. "And now?"

"Now we're going to a planetary exit." Telzey touched a point in the captive mind. "That hidden one you people installed. . . . Set up a route through empty sections, and unseal that series of portals."

The planetary exit portal opened on an enclosed courtyard. Four aircars stood in a row along one wall. Telzey paused at the exit beside Kolki Ming, looking around. It appeared to be early morning in that part of Tinokti. They were on the fringes of a city; buildings stretched away in the distance. There were city sounds, vague and remote.

She glanced down at herself. She'd washed hands, face and hair on the way, but hadn't been able to get her clothing clean. It didn't show; she'd fastened a wide shawl of bright-colored fabric around herself, a strip they'd cut from tapestry in one of the circuit sections. It concealed the blood and dirt stains on her clothes, and the Elaigar knife at her belt.

She adjusted the shawl, looked up at the immensely formidable creature beside her. The Alatta's eyes returned her gaze without expression. Telzey started forward toward the cars. Kolki Ming stayed where she was. Telzey climbed into the nearest of the cars, checked the controls. The interior was designed to Sparan proportions, otherwise this was standard equipment. She could handle it. She unlocked the engine, turned it on. A red alert light appeared, then faded as the invisble energy field above the court dissolved to let her through.

She swung the car about, lifted it from the ground, moved up out of the court. Two hundred yards away, she spun the viewscreen dial to focus on the motionless figure by the portal. The car drove up and on in a straight line. When the figure began to dwindle in the screen, Telzey abruptly withdrew her holds from Kolki Ming's mind, slammed her own shield tight, remembering their lightning reflexes.

But nothing happened. Kolki Ming remained where

she was for a moment, seemed to be looking after her. Then she turned aside, disappeared through the portal.

Five minutes later, Telzey brought the car down in a public parking area, left it there with locked engine and doors. The entrance to a general transportation circuit fronted on the parking space. She went inside, oriented herself on the circuit maps, and set out. Not long afterwards, she exited near a large freight spaceport.

21

The freight port adjoined a run-down city area with a population which lived in the main on Tongi Phon handouts. It had few attractions and an oversupply of predators. Otherwise, it was a good place for somebody who wanted to drop out of sight.

Telzey let a thoroughly vicious pair of predators, one of them a young woman of about her size, trail her along the main streets for a while. They were uncomplicated mentalities, readily accessible. She turned at last into a narrow alley, and when they caught up with her there, they were her robots. She exchanged street clothes with the woman in a deserted backyard, left the alley with the Elaigar knife wrapped in a cloth she'd taken from a trash pile. The two went on in the opposite direction, the woman carrying the folded length of tapestry she'd coveted. Their minds had been provided with a grim but plausible account of how she'd come by it and the blood-stained expensive clothing she now wore.

Telzey stopped at a nearby store she'd learned about from them. The store paid cash for anything salable; and when she left it a few minutes later, it had the Elaigar knife and she had a pocketful of Tinokti coins. It wasn't much money but enough for her immediate needs. An hour later, she'd rented a room above a small store for a week, locked the door, and unpacked the few items she'd picked up. One of them was a recorder. She turned it on, stretched out on the narrow bed.

It was high time. Part of her mind had been called upon to do more than was healthy for it in these hours, and it was now under noticeable strain. There were flickerings of distorted thought, emotional surges, impulses born in other minds and reproduced in her own. She'd been keeping it under control because she had to. Tolant and Tanven, Elaigar and Alatta, Thrakell Dees —Phon Dees once, a lord of the circuit, and in the end, its last human survivor—they'd all been packed in under her recent personal experiences which were crammed and jolting enough. She'd lived something of the life of each in their memories, and she had to get untangled from that before there were permanent effects.

She let the stream of borrowed impressions start boiling through into consciousness, sorting them over as they came, drained off emotional poisons. Now and then, she spoke into the recorder. That was for the Psychology Service; there were things they should know. Other things might be useful for her to remember privately. They went back now into mental storage, turned into neat, neutral facts—knowledge. Much of the rest was valueless, had been picked up incidentally. It could be sponged from her mind at once, and was, became nonexistent.

The process continued; pressures began to reduce. The first two days she had nightmares when she slept, felt depressed while awake. Then her mood lightened. She ate when hungry, exercised when she felt like it, went on putting her mental house back in order. By the sixth day, as recorded by the little calendar watch she'd bought, she was done. Her experiences with the Elaigar, from the first contact in Melna Park on, were put in perspective, had become a thing of the past, no longer to concern her.

Back to normal. . . .

She spent the last few hours of the day working over her report to the Psychology Service, and had her first night of unbroken sleep in a week. Early next morning, she slipped the recorder into her pocket, unlocked the door, went whistling softly down to the store. The storekeeper, who had just opened up, gave her a puzzled look and scratched his chin. He was wondering how it could have completely slipped his mind all week that he had a renter upstairs. Telzey smiled amiably at him, went out into the street. He stared after her a moment, then turned away and forgot the renter again, this time for good.

Telzey walked on half a block, relaxed her screens and sent an identification thought to her Service contacts. A Service squad was there four minutes later to pick her up.

"There's somebody else," Klayung told her eventually, "who'd like to speak to you about your report." This was two days later, and they were in a service ship standing off Tinokti.

"Who is it this time?" Telzey inquired warily. She'd had a number of talks with Klayung and a few other Service people about her experiences in the Elaigar circuit. Within limits, she hadn't minded giving them more detailed information than the report provided, but she was beginning to feel that for the moment she'd been pumped enough.

"He's a ranking official of a department which had a supporting role in the operation," Klayung said. "For security reasons, he doesn't want his identity to be known."

"I see. What about my identity?" Klayung had been very careful to keep Telzey unidentified so far. The role she'd played on Tinokti was known, in varying degrees, only to a few dozen members of the Service, to Neto Nayne-Mel who was at present in Service therapy, and to the Alattas, who no longer mattered.

"We'll have you camouflaged during the discussion," Klayung said. "You'll talk by viewscreen."

"I suppose he isn't satisfied with the report?" Telzey said.

"No. He feels it doesn't go far enough and suspects you're holding things back deliberately. He's also unhappy about your timing."

She considered. It made no difference now. "He doesn't know about the part with Neto, does he?"

"No. Except for you and the therapists and a few others like myself, there was no Neto Nayne-Mel in the circuit."

"Shall I be frank with him otherwise?"

"Within reason," said Klayung.

She found herself sitting shortly before a viewscreen, with Klayung in the room behind her. The official at the other screen wore a full face mask. He might as well have left it off. She knew who he was as soon as he started to speak. They'd met on Orado.

She wasn't wearing a mask. Klayung's make-up people had put in half an hour preparing her for the meeting. What the official saw and heard was an undersized middle-aged man with a twang to his voice.

The discussion began on a polite if cool note. Telzey was informed that the circuit she'd described had been located that morning. The force fields about the individual sections had all cut off simultaneously. After an entry into one of the sections was effected, it was discovered there was no need for the special portal keys with which she'd provided the Service. The entire system was now as open as any general circuit on Tinokti. Exploration remained cautious until it became obvious that the portal traps of which she'd spoken had been destructured. Nor was anything left which might have provided a clue to the device referred to in the report as the Vingarran Gate. "And, needless to say," said the official, "no one was found in the circuit."

Telzey nodded. "They've been gone for a week now. They set the force fields to shut off after it was safe, so you could stop looking for them."

"Meanwhile," the official went on, "we've had verification enough for your statement that groups of these aliens, both the Alattas and the Elaigar, were masquerading as human giants throughout the Federation. They've even owned considerable property. One well-known shipping line ostensibly was bought up by a Sparan organization three years ago and thereafter operated exclusively by Sparans. We know now that's not what they were. All these groups have vanished. Every positive lead we've traced reveals the same story. They disappeared within less than a standard day of one another, leaving nothing behind to indicate where they came from or where they've gone."

"That was the Alatta plan," Telzey acknowledged. "They wanted it to be a fast, clean break and a complete one."

"It seems," the official said, "you had this information in your possession a week before you chose to reveal it. I'm wondering, of course, what made you assume the responsibility of allowing the aliens to escape."

"For one thing, there wasn't much time," Telzey said. "If the Alatta operation was delayed, the situation would change—they wouldn't be able to carry out their plan as they'd intended. For another, I wasn't sure everyone here would understand what the situation was. I wanted them to be out of the Hub with the Elaigar before somebody made the wrong decision."

"And what makes you sure you made the right one?" the official demanded. "You may have saved us trouble at the moment while setting us up for much more serious trouble in the future."

She shook her head.

"They're not coming back," she said. "If they did, we'd spot them, now that we know about them. But the Elaigar won't be able to come back, and the Alattas don't want to. They think it will be better if there's no further contact at all between them and the Federation for a good long time to come."

"How do you know?"

"I looked through the mind of one of them," Telzey said. "That was one of the things I had to know, of course."

The official regarded her a moment.

"In looking through that Alatta's mind, you must have picked up some impression of their galactic locations. . . ."

"No, I didn't," Telzey said. "I was careful not to. I didn't want to know that."

"Why not?" There was an edge of exasperation to his voice.

"Because *I* think it will be much better if there's no further contact between us for a good long time. From either side."

The face mask shifted slightly, turning in Klayung's direction.

"Dr. Klayung," said the official, "with all the devices at the Service's disposal, there must be some way of determining whether this man has told us the full truth!"

Klayung scratched his chin.

"Knowing him as I do," he said, "I'm sure that if he felt he might be forced to reveal something he didn't wish to reveal, he'd simply wipe the matter from his mind. And we'd get nothing. So we might as well accept his statement. The Service is quite willing to do it."

"In that case," the official said, "there seems to be no point in continuing this talk."

"I had the impression," Klayung remarked, as he left the communication room with Telzey, "that you knew who he was."

Telzey nodded. "I do. Ramadoon. How'd he get involved in this? I thought he was only a Council Deputy."

"He fills a number of roles, depending on circumstances," Klayung told her. "A valuable man. Excellent organizer, highly intelligent, with a total loyalty to the Federation."

"And very stubborn," Telzey added. "I think he plans to put in a lot of effort now to get that psi in the Tinokti circuit identified."

"No doubt," said Klayung. "But it won't be long before that slips from his mind again."

"It will? Well, good! Then I won't have to worry about it. I can see why he might feel I've put the Federation at a disadvantage."

"Haven't you?"

"You didn't believe I don't know where the Alatta territories are, did you?"

"No," Klayung said. "We assumed you'd bring up that subject eventually."

"Well, I'm telling the Service, of course. But I thought we'd wait until things settle down again all around. I got a good general impression, but it will take mapping specialists and plenty of time to pinpoint it. They must be way off our charts. And that," Telzey added, "technically will put the Alattas at a disadvantage then."

"I'm not sure I follow you," Klayung said.

"The way the Alattas have worked it out, the human psis of the times, and especially the variations in them, had a good deal to do with defeating the Elaigar at Nalakia."

"Hmmm!" Klayung rubbed his jaw. "We've no record of that—but there would be none on our side, of course. An interesting speculation!"

"They don't think it's speculation. They're all psis, but they're all the same general kind of psi. They're born that way; it's part of the mutation. They don't change. They know we vary a lot and that we do change. That's why they wanted to take me along and analyze me. I'm pretty close to the Elaigar type of psi myself at present, but they figured there was more to it than that."

"Well," Klayung said, "you may have proved the point to their satisfaction now. The disadvantage, incidentally, will remain a technical one. The Service also feels contacts between the Federation and the Alattas would be quite undesirable in any foreseeable future."

They were passing a reflecting bulkhead as he spoke, and Telzey caught a sudden glimpse of herself. The middle-aged little man in the bulkhead grimaced distastefully at her. Her gaze shifted to a big wall clock at the end of the passageway, showing Tongi Phon and standard time and dates.

She calculated a moment.

"Klayung," she said, "does the Service owe me a favor?"

Klayung's expression became a trifle cautious. "Why, I'd say we're under considerable obligation to you. What favor did you have in mind?"

"Will you have Make-up turn me back like I was right away?"

"Of course. And?"

"Can you put me on a ship that's fast enough to get me to Orado City this evening, local time?"

Klayung glanced at the clock, calculated briefly in turn.

"I'm sure that can be arranged," he said then. He looked curiously at her. "Is there some special significance to the time you arrive there?"

"Not to me so much," Telzey said. "But I just remembered—today's my birthday. I'm sixteen, and the family wants me to be home for the party."

About the Author. . . .

James Henry Schmitz was born in Hamburg, Germany in 1911 of American parents, and moved to the U.S. in 1938. He worked in harvester and trailer building, first in Germany and then in the U.S., and served with the U.S.A.F. in the Pacific during World War II. In 1959 he turned to a full-time writing career. His first published science fiction story, "Greenface", appeared in *Unknown* in 1943. In the 1960s, when the majority of his novels were written and published, Mr. Schmitz firmly established himself as one of the leading writers in the field. He is perhaps best known for his delightful novel *The Witches of Karres,* and for his consistent use of strong female protagonists at a time when science fiction was a male-oriented genre.